# Eight.

Katie Salyer

Eight.

Katie Salyer

ISBN # 978-1-5151-0879-5

First trade paperback edition December 2015

Interior design by Katie Salyer

Front and back cover design by J. Tyler Provence

Manufactured in the United States.

Business Email: KatieSalyerWrites@gmail.com⬚

To Allen Salyer,
Rest easy, Uncie. I'll see you when I get where I'm
going…
11/2/1968-10/26/2006


This is the first book I have ever written.
I began writing this on May 25th, 2013 on my iPhone.

# one
## Kaili

Eight.

That number and I have a love-hate relationship. I was eight when Dad bought me my first puppy. Mom and Dad had been married for eight years when I was born. My brother is two years and eight months older than me. And it only takes eight steps to get from the front door to the basement door.

"One, two, three, four, five..." I counted the booted steps above me.

"Six, seven, eight..."

My heart pounded and I tried to control my shaky breathing. I heard a low growl above me and the basement door swung open and crashed into the wall.

My body tensed and a bag of bread was thrown towards me. It must be the beginning of a new month. That's the only time I am ever given food.

The door slammed closed and I jolted in fear. I prayed and waited until I heard the footsteps get quieter and quieter.

I shifted and rose from my position on the floor and slowly stepped towards the food. I opened it and smelled it, allowing myself to smile. Fresh bread always smelled the best. I closed the bag and tied it tightly to store it for later. As I laid down my food, I heard what sounded like a motorcycle rush by. Where

I am, I'm not sure. All I know is that I was put here when I was ten years old and have been here for nearly eight years.

There's another reason I hate eight.

The desk under the stairs caught my eye and I walked over to it. I picked up the razor blade on top of it and used it to carve a tally mark into the wood. I use the tally marks to tell me how long I've been down here. Today makes 98 months in here, which is a month short of eight years. I'm not sure what month it is. I forgot what they were all called except October because that's my birthday month. But I do know there's twelve of them in one year.

The window has been cracked for as long as I can remember, but the wooden boards nailed across it are fairly new. Every now and then, I can hear cars driving by. I wish he wouldn't have used so many boards on it. Now I can't even see outside. I guess trying to get out through the window wasn't my smartest move, but who could blame me? I wanted out. I never wanted in, really. I just wish I knew why he picked me.

My life wasn't always this way. Before I was taken, I was a military daughter. Chief Petty Officer Jason Taylor of the United States Navy is my father. I'm not entirely sure what my father does in the Navy, but I'm a well aware of his importance. He was about to be deployed to Thailand when I was taken.

My mom, Emily, is an English teacher for military base high schools. She is a very smart woman and I miss her so much.

I lived on base with my family in Florida. Our house was fancy since Dad made so much money. We lived on the same street as many of the officers and their families.

I also have one sibling; my older brother Mark. He's my best friend. He had a passion for music that was unexplainable although I was the only one he ever really sang for.

Being a military family, we traveled quite a bit with my dad. We had lived in California, Texas, Washington State, Virginia, and even Japan for a short time. Throughout all of this, the only friend I've ever really had was my brother. Sure we fought like a normal brother and sister would, but he was the only person I could really trust besides Mom and Dad.

After we moved to Florida, our schooling wasn't going to start for another month so we went on a road trip. We were going to go to California to see Disneyland with another military family based in San Diego, but my vacation was cut short in Nevada at a rest area. That's when it happened.

I was snapped out of my depressing thoughts upon hearing water moving through the pipes above me. I ran a finger under my eyes, wiping away any tears that had brimmed over. I sniffled and took a deep breath. In hopes to clear my mind, I looked around my dark home and soon realized that I was not alone.

He had somehow made his way down the stairs without me noticing. My heart started its usual routine of beating out of my chest in fear. He stood in front of me with a baseball bat in his hands. He used this on me many times, so I was used to it. His face stretched into a smile and he raised it above his head. Instinctively, I flinched and crouched down to the floor. Covering my face, I waited for the attack to begin.

You can imagine my surprise when he dropped the bat at my feet. The metal clanked against the concrete and rolled closer to me. My arms were held close to my body and my legs were tucked under my chin. I looked up at him and he tapped his foot.

"I don't want to beat you yet. Use it on the mice. I'll be back if I hear you trying to get out again. Understood?" His deep voice tore through me and I nodded quickly. He tilted his head to the side and his eyes squinted. I stayed on the floor, trying to keep from crying in front of him. Crying only made him angrier.

He forcefully grabbed my arm and lifted me to my feet.

"Speak." He got in my face and held my arm tighter.

"Yes sir," I whimpered and he let go of my arm. His eyes lowered down my body and he smiled.

"That's my good girl." His hand reached up and touched my face. I felt the tears falling and his hand gripped my jaw. I let out a yelp and he held tighter. His other hand reared back and slapped my cheek with enough force to send me tumbling to the floor.

"I told you not to cry in front of me," he yelled, standing over me. I tried as hard as I could to stop crying but it was so hard. He's beaten me hundreds of times, but it's never gotten easier or less scary. Him standing over me like this is an everyday thing but the fear will never die down. This man will forever haunt my dreams and I don't even know his name.

He stood straight and headed back up the steps, leaving me alone again. I heard the door slam shut and the locks clicking. I touched my face and the skin was hot. My face was numb and my ankle was bruising and swelling from landing on it wrong. I tried to stand up but failed, falling back to the ground. I scooted across the floor, propped myself up against the wall, and finally let myself cry.

I spent a few minutes just letting my emotions out. Very quietly, of course. I've spent many days like this. My mom once told me, "You're not weak if you cry every once in a while," and I have tried to remember that every day I've spent sobbing into my busted knees. I know I'm physically weak. There's no question about it. But as far as mentally, I'd say I'm pretty strong. At least I hope I am. If I'm not, I'll just keep telling myself I am until it's true.

The cold medal of my necklace touched my chest. I looked down and pulled it out of my shirt. I replayed in my mind the day I had received this necklace. It was my father's military tags he had asked me to hold while we were in Nevada. He handed it to me while he and Mark were playing basketball in the parking lot. "Hold on to this for me, Kaili. It's very important that you keep it safe," he told me. His large hands held it above my head and he swiftly draped it over my shoulders, letting the cool medallion slide down my shirt.

I shook my head, ending my flashback. A tear fell from my cheek and landed on the tag. Wiping it off with my thumb, I placed the necklace back in my shirt for safe keeping. That was the only reminder of home I had besides memories. It was the small spec of hope my fragile heart still had.

# two
## Kaili

Two weeks of trying to eat a little without eating all of my food went by. My ankle was still swollen and bruised, but I could walk on it now. He beat me every day, just like usual. This morning, he passed out while beating me and I stayed far away from him when he woke up. He was fine but I wasn't. I had a few new bruises and cuts, but nothing major. He hadn't raped me in the last two months, which was somewhat promising. He usually rapes me a few times a month, but he hasn't. Maybe he's getting bored with me.

Just as I was letting a small smile grace my tired face, a mouse ran across the floor. He ran behind, around, and under everything in the basement, looking for a way out. I knew he would find one eventually, but I had hoped he wouldn't. It was almost fun watching him run around. His little legs carried him all around the basement. He leaped behind the large stack of boxes and I heard him squeak.

Knowing what it felt like to be trapped, I was determined to help the little creature. I walked slowly to the boxes and started moving them out of the way. I found him stuck between a mirror and the wall.

"How did you get stuck in there, little guy?" I asked, knowing he didn't understand. He squeaked and looked up at me with terrified eyes. I moved the mirror and he moved as fast as his little legs could carry him. He leaped over boxes and climbed up onto the pipes along the ceiling. He found the hole in the window and shot through it, leaving me alone once again.

*Dang it.*

My gaze went back to the mirror and I lifted it slowly and carried it away from the boxes. *Why hadn't I noticed this down here before?* It was dusty, old, and cracked in a few places and looked to have lipstick smudged on it. It must have been a teenage girl's mirror at one point. I wiped away some of the dust with my hand and looked at my reflection.

I had almost forgotten what I look like. I'm rather short, my clothes ripped and dirty. They aren't really my clothes. I found these clothes in one of the boxes down here a few months ago and I've been wearing them ever since. My once brown hair is now knotted and ratty and grayish. My once tan skin is now scarred, bruised, and pale. Some of the cuts I did, but most of them were from him. I had a small scar on my neck from when I was kidnapped. He had cut me several times in attempt to kill me that day.

I looked at my face and lightly touched the big bruises. My lip and forehead are cut. I looked into my green eyes and saw terror and exhaustion. I felt tears streaming down my cheeks as my eyes traveled to my stomach. It looked larger than usual, and I knew it wasn't a result of being over fed. I raised my shirt and looked at my stomach in the mirror. I looked down and studied my tummy before touching it. It felt funny, like it was full.

14

Fear nearly stopped my heart. I tried to think of any reason as to why my stomach was swollen, but I couldn't think of anything. I dropped to my knees and cried into my hands.

"How am I supposed to take care of myself down here?" I thought out loud. I need to get out of here. I can't die down here. *This isn't how it ends.*

I sat on the ground and thought of different ways I could escape. I've tried everything there was to try and always failed. I've tried picking the locks, which resulted in a beating. I've tried breaking the window, which resulted in rape. I've tried to dig my way out, but I'm surrounded by concrete and wood above me. And I've even tried to kill myself, but I'm too weak to actually do it. My body isn't strong enough to do even the simplest of tasks. I know I'm helpless, but I'm very hopeful.

"How, God? How am I supposed to get away?" I spoke quietly.

Almost instantly, I heard a door swing open. It never shut, which means he's drunk. Normally, I would be shaking with fear right now. But not today. I knew God had given me an escape.

I stood up confidently and waited for my attacker to come down the stairs and begin his beating. I knew his every move. I knew exactly where he'd hit me and where he wouldn't. And I knew I could take it one more time.

The past eight years of fear and pain left my mind, replaced with gleaming hope. All I heard in my mind were the words "scream, child," and I knew it was God speaking to me. I nodded my head in response to the words swimming around my mind. I reached behind me and grabbed the baseball bat and held it strong.

I heard the heavy steps approach the basement door and it swung open. I started screaming as loud as I could in hopes of someone hearing me. He revealed himself at the top of the stair case. With anger written all over his face and alcohol running through his veins, he let out a horrible growl. He stumbled down the stairs and ran towards me, taking a swing.

I screamed as loud as I could and his fist connected with my arm. He was still too drunk to hit me properly, which has happened before. I smashed the baseball bat over his head and he grabbed it from me. The hit must have woke him up a bit, because he quickly became furious.

I heard more footsteps above my head and I screamed louder than ever before. He pulled a knife out of his pocket and started slashing at my legs and ran it across the small of my back. I grabbed the knife out of his hands and threw it away from us. His fist smashed into my left eye and I blacked out as I hit the ground.

# three
## Mark

My fingers were interlocked, elbows resting on my knees as I hunched over, sitting on an overpriced, poorly built couch. I took in a deep breath and looked around my hotel room. It was fancy, much like something The President of the United States would stay in. My manager, Lia, sat across from me typing away contently on her laptop. She spent most of her time on that thing, ignoring the world around her as she worked. She's not rude. That's just who she is.

I grabbed my iPhone, unlocked it, and looked at the background picture. It was taken at a rest stop in Nevada eight years ago. I smiled and felt a tear run down my cheek and land on the screen. The picture was of me, my mom, my dad, and Kaili. My sister. My best friend. My biggest fan. The reason I am on a headlining world tour at this very moment.

Ever since I got my first cell phone, that picture has been my background. I've had a few girlfriends, but none of them meant more to me than my family. Even Natalie knows she ranks under this picture. She accepts it, which is one of the many reasons I love her so much.

I looked down at my wrist and ran my finger over the ink. The tattoo is only two inches long and I'm the only one who knows what it means. To everyone else, it's an infinity sign. But in all reality, it's an eight. That's my number. I was eight when my dad told me we were moving back to America from Japan, I've broken eight bones, I have eight Grammys, and my sister has been gone for eight years.

She was the only one who had heard me sing growing up. She encouraged me to pursue music, but I lacked confidence in myself. She knew everything there was to know about me and all of my success is dedicated to her, wherever she is. She was taken from us in Nevada by a man I had never seen before. She was grabbed and thrown into the back of his truck in a matter of seconds. We tried so hard to find her but it was nearly impossible considering the man covered his face and license plate.

A week after the kidnapping, my father was deployed to Thailand. He was killed a few weeks later in a jetfighter crash. The news was heart breaking.

My mother went crazy. She started using drugs and stole things from many different places. She was so depressed that she ended her life a short time after Dad died. I remember feeling so alone and confused. I lived with my grandparents until the day I turned eighteen. On my eighteenth birthday, I caught the first flight to California to start my music career.

After living a few months on the streets, I met my best friend Tanner on Sunset Boulevard. One day while I was busking on the streets, he stopped and watched me play my guitar and sing. He stayed around for about an hour listening to me play classic rock and newer pop music before finally speaking to me. He didn't say much. The only words he said to me in the beginning were, "You're pretty good, man".

After that, we became really close. He would come to that small corner every day to listen to me play. He told me he could make things happen for me in the music industry, which I found far-fetched. Little did I know, Tanner's father owned the building of a big name record company.

I was brutally snapped out of my thoughts when a pillow hit my face. I looked away from my phone and saw Lia's foot tapping impatiently on the floor in front of me.

"Come on, you only have two hours until the concert," she instructed, holding her coffee and laptop. I nodded and hopped off the couch and headed for the shower. This is the only alone time I ever really have, so I cherish it.

I often wonder where Kaili is, if she's alive, what she looks like, how much she has changed, if I would ever see her again. I pray every night that one day I will be reunited with her.

My fans know about her. It amazes me how they can find out my phone number and my blood type but they can't find my sister. The kidnapper must have her in a strange country or something.

I refuse to lose hope on finding my sister. I sing for her every day. She's the reason I get up on stage and sing my heart out. She's the inspiration behind every performance. Every dollar earned is in her name. God put her on Earth for a reason and I refuse to believe that it was to be kidnapped.

After sound check, it was show time in Las Vegas. I walked on stage with my head down and heard the fans screaming. I felt the energy and the excitement in the stadium. I smiled and looked around the arena. Thousands of teenage girls were squealing and a few fainted when I walked passed them.

This is normal for me. Some of my fans held signs with naughty and vulgar phrases written on them, some mentioning an inside joke within the fandom, and some saying I shouldn't lose hope on finding Kaili. On stage is the only place I feel connected with her. It's almost like she's out there listening, although I am almost certain that that is impossible.

I took a deep breath and grabbed my guitar. I waved a hello to my adoring fans and began singing. I zoned out, losing myself in the music. I closed my eyes to hit the highest notes. Confidence was something I had never possessed, but being on that stage is different. It feels natural.

I feel a connection with all these kids and my crew. They are my world. They never lost faith in me. They never left. They didn't forget about me when a new star came around. They stuck with me like a family would, which is something I haven't had in a long time.

# four
## Andrew

Today is my last day working for this stupid company, I swear it. I swear it every day, but I mean it this time. I *hate* being a mailman. I hate being chased by dogs, having cats attack me, and being cursed at for knocking on peoples doors when it's their own fault for not having a real mailbox. It's all a load of horse shit.

I grabbed the mailbox door in front of me and stuffed the mail inside, slamming it shut.

The dog across the yard started barking at me viciously and I couldn't help but laugh. It was a miniature poodle. *What's a poodle going to do to me? Yap me to death? Ha.* I flipped the dog off and turned back to my piece-of-crap mail truck, jumping inside.

An old beat up Chevy pulled in across the street from me and parked in the driveway. I smelled alcohol and a man stumbled out of the vehicle, tripping over his feet. He was clearly drunk and oddly frightening. He turned towards me and smirked at me. I sat as still as possible as he turned back to the house and walked towards the front door. I watched as he took the last swig of Jack Daniels and threw the empty bottle on the lawn. *Damn. I wish I could have had some.*

He swung the front door open and left it. I heard a blood-curdling scream and instantly froze. *Oh shit*. I leaned forward and listened closely just to make sure I wasn't about to do something incredibly crazy.

I heard more screams and what sounded like someone being hit with something. My heart started pounding harder and harder. I knew good and well that I would never be able to stop someone from being beaten to death, so I settled on the idea of calling someone.

My shaky hand reached in my pocket and grabbed my phone. Of course my dispatcher would never believe me, so I called 911. I pressed my phone to my ear and paced back and forth, waiting for someone to answer. Finally, a woman spoke.

"911, what's your emergency?"

"Hi. Umm, I think someone is being beaten in the house across from me." I shook my hand violently while I spoke, trying to calm down as I heard another scream.

"Where are you located, sir?" Another scream.

"Uhh, 5329 South Rose Street. It's an old house with a bunch of beer bottles in the lawn. Please hurry. It sounds like a young girl in there."

I heard another almost beastlike growl and a scream.

"Okay, sir, we are sending police out now. Please stay calm and wait for the police to handle it."

"But what if they don't get here soon enough? Oh forget it..." A burst of adrenaline and courage shot through me like electricity. I dropped my phone in the grass and ran towards the house. I ran inside and my heart pounded harder with every step I took.

"This place is so shifty," I whispered to myself.

I found a bunch of old baseball bat by the door, grabbed one, and looked for the source of the screaming. I stumbled down a set of wooden stairs at the end of a hallway to a basement. When I reached the bottom, I found the man with his back to me, beating a young girl senseless. She was unconscious and had several bruises and gashes all over her body.

My protective instincts kicked in and I took a swing at the man with the bat. The aluminum connected with the man's lower back and he growled in pain, falling to the ground. I stood over him and he passed out; more than likely from too much alcohol.

I looked over at the young girl and took a deep breath. I crouched over her body and placed my hand on her wrist, checking for a heartbeat. Her veins pulsed under my touch and relief washed over me.

I sat down beside her body and held her up in my hands and my mind wandered off to a dark place that not many people know about.

When I was younger, my little sister Kelly and I were swimming in a creek that Mom told us to stay away from. There was a steep hill that we had to climb up to get away from the creek, but she didn't make it up. She ended up tumbling down the hill and I had to hold her head above water while screaming for Mom. I remember thinking she was dead.

Mom found us and took us to the hospital. Kelly had a concussion and a broken rib. Mom got onto me a lot that day. Although she apologized later for it, I know she still blames me for the accident. It was my fault and I hated myself for taking Kelly to that creek.

Shaking the memory away, I quickly noticed that the girl was bleeding all over the floor. Her legs were covered in cuts and I felt blood on my hand. I pulled it out from under her back and gasped, quickly placing it back where it was. Hopefully whatever I'm doing is helping. I'd hate to have this random girl I've never seen before die in my arms.

I heard police sirens coming towards the house and stop in what I was assuming was the front yard. I yelled for the police to help them find us. Five officers ran down the stairs with guns pointed at me and I kept in my whimper at the sight. I stuck my hands up and stood up slowly.

"I called 911," I announced, still shaking because of what had happened just moments before.

One officer pointed his gun down at the attacker laying on the floor and touched the man's arm with his foot.

"He's unconscious, sir," another officer commented.

"Is she breathing?" The first officer asked. I nodded and pointed at the baseball bat I had used.

"I hit him. He was gonna kill her," I stammered.

"Good job, bud. Come on. I'll call a medic and get her to a hospital. Poor girl looks like she's been down here for years," the oldest officer of the five observed. I nodded and took one more look at the girl before following him up the steps.

We waited for a while before the paramedic arrived and got the girl out of the basement safely. She was being sent to a hospital. The attacker, on the other hand, was being taken to jail. Apparently he has been on the wanted list for the past twelve years. My body tensed when every warrant the man had was read to me by the officer. Trespassing. Robbery. Even attempted murder was on the list. *This is insane.*

I was being taken to the police station for more questioning and one of the paramedics was going to let me know if the girl was going to be okay. On the way there, I called my boss to let him know what was happening. Next, I called Kelly who's also a police officer to tell her everything.

"Hello?" She answered.

"Hey Kells. You won't believe what just happened." A bunch of static was coming through the phone, which meant her pager was going off.

"Hang on, there's a kidnapping report coming in," she told me.

"Yeah I know. I was the one who found her," I revealed, looking out of the windshield at the ambulance in front of us.

"No way!" My sister gasped.

"Yeah I was on my mail route and this guy pulled into the house across from me. He was clearly drunk and really creepy looking. Anyway, he left his front door opened and I heard this awful screaming coming from inside the house. So I called 911 and just ran inside and somehow ended up in the basement. I don't know. The entire thing was sketchy. All I remember is hitting the guy with a bat and him passing out and seeing the girl unconscious on the floor. It was crazy."

My breathing was rushed and shallow as I relived the event. I could feel my blood pressure spiking and I took deep breaths. Her scream is a sound I won't soon forget.

"Wow. You did good, Andy. Really good. Maybe the chief will assign me to her case so I can keep you updated on her. Legally, of course," she praised me.

"I would appreciate it. It looked like she'd been down there forever. I wonder if she's Mark Taylor's sister. Ya know, the one who went missing like eight years ago that he always talks about? Wouldn't that be something?" I couldn't help but hope it was his sister. I couldn't imagine losing mine.

"It could be. You never know. Hey I gotta go to the station. I'll see ya down there in a bit, okay? Love you, Bub." Kelly and I said our goodbyes and I hung up. When I looked up, we had just arrived at the station with the crazy man in the car behind us.

# five
## Mark

My thumbs ghosted over the game controller buttons as I waited for Tanner to press play.

"Dude I'm totally gonna kill you," he talked trash, sitting down on the other end of the couch. I rolled my eyes and he pressed play. The beginning credits of NBA 2K13 displayed on the tour bus TV and my mind clicked into game mode.

Nearly two hours passed by as the bus drove down the road. I watched as Tanner's player shot a three-pointer and sunk it, winning the game. He jumped up and did a victory dance and I grunted, sitting my controller aside and looking at my phone. I looked at the picture of my family and felt Tanner looking over at me.

"Mark, you've got to quit staring at that picture. I know it hurts man but you have to stop depressing yourself," he scolded, sitting back down beside me. I nodded and wiped away an escaped tear with my thumb.

Tanner knows everything about Kaili. I told him before I got famous, and he's helped me through so much. Sure, everything happened a long time ago, but it's not just something you can forget about.

The bus slowed to a stop and I looked out the window. We were outside the Staples Center in downtown LA. Tanner and I stepped off the bus and a black Range Rover pulled up. The window rolled down and I was met by a fake smile and an awful bowtie on my publicist.

"Let's go! You have an interview with Justin Stewart in an hour!" He yelled, rolling his window up. Justin Stewart was the first radio host to interview me and we've been pals ever since. He's been one of the very few people I've been able to trust since I was signed to the record label.

I ran back on the bus and grabbed my guitar and phone. Tanner, Lia, and I got in the Range Rover and drove to the radio station in silence.

The interview was like every interview I've done. Same people, same questions, same answers.

"Are you dating anyone?"

"How is Natalie doing?"

"Have you popped the question?"

"Have you two broken up?"

"What are your plans for after the tour?"

*Blah blah blah.*

I answered all of them as truthfully as I could and Justin asked me to sing something acoustic. I sang a few songs and answered more questions from fans who had called in. Most of the questions involved marriage proposals or something to that extent. I honestly don't understand what all the fuss is about. I thought the questions were over until a young girl called in from Texas.

"Hey you're on with Mark Taylor! What's your name, sweetie?" Justin asked.

"Oh my gosh! No way!" She squealed.

"What's your name, hon?" I asked, smiling at her excitement.

"Cierra." Her voice sounded shaky.

"Hey Cierra! What's your question, babe?"

"If you could say one thing to your sister now, what would it be?"

I fell silent at the question. Everyone in the studio looked at me with questioning eyes. Tanner gave me a reassuring look and I felt tears building in my eyes.

"We can skip the question," Justin whispered, covering the mic so he couldn't be heard on the air. I shook my head, refusing to ignore a fan's question. I looked at my feet and thought long and hard. Taking a deep breath, I finally answered her.

"I, uhh, I don't really know what I would say to Kaili exactly. I would probably tell her that I miss her so much and can't wait for the day I'll see her again," I answered truthfully, voice wavering. No one in the industry ever brought up Kaili. I had refused to answer anything about her for her sake and mine. It had been over a year since anyone asked me about her in an interview.

Justin ended the interview and I thanked him before walking out of the studio. As the door slammed behind me, I quickened my pace. I knew eventually someone would chase after me, but I didn't care. I heard the door of the building swing open again and my legs moved quicker.

"Bro, wait up!" I heard Tanner's voice plead. I shook my head and continued to walk down the alley behind the studio. My hands held the back of my head and I watched my feet carry me further. Tears began to steadily stream down my face.

I hate talking about my sister. It kills me.

Tanner's footsteps continued to follow me and I knew there was no use in trying to run from him. I stopped and leaned my back against the building beside the studio. The cool brick soothed me as I wiped away tears from my face. I dropped to the ground and brought my knees up to my chest, covering my face with my hands.

I felt my best friend hovering over me. His hand touched my shoulder and I proceeded to break down. Tears ran unmercifully from my eyes and I tried to calm myself down. Tanner sat down beside me and put his arm around my shoulder. He took a deep breath before speaking.

"Look man, I'm not gonna pretend I know what's going through your head right now because I don't. I have no idea what this feels like for you. But believe me when I say that we will find Kaili. She's out there somewhere. I can feel it. I know it's been eight years and all but you can't lose hope. She's out there. I don't know why, but I can feel it."

"I don't know, dude. She could be dead for all I know."

"You can't think like that, Mark. I know she's out there. I don't know where, but something's telling me she is." His hand gripped my shoulder and shook it softly.

"What the hell makes you think that?" I snapped and nudged his hand off of me.

"I told you I don't know, alright? I just feel it. It's almost like a hunch."

I rolled my eyes at him and huffed. He's right. I can't lose hope. But I can't help but think of the worst considering how long it's been since I've seen her. I knew Tanner well enough that when he has a hunch, I listen. It may be hard to believe, but in the end he is almost always right. I was just terrified that, this time, he might not be.

"Did you take your anxiety medicine this morning?" His voice was guarded. I had been on anxiety medication for two years now. This 'famous' life isn't the easiest, and my past doesn't exactly help.

"Yeah. Talking about Kaili gives me anxiety, though. You know that." I lifted my hands and watched them shake. Tanner nodded his head and took a deep breath.

"One of these days you're going to be off those pills, man," he assured me.

I let out a little laugh and he looked over at me.

"I'm serious. One of these days, everything is going to sort itself out. You'll have your sister back. You'll find out where she's been all these years. And you'll be the happy, ambitious Mark Taylor I met three years ago on Sunset," he smiled, throwing his arm around me in a brotherly way. I smiled over at him and nodded my head.

"What's the one thing that helps with your anxiety the most?" He asked, standing up and brushing off his jeans.

"Music," I retorted. He stuck his hand out to help me up and I took it, pulling myself off the ground.

"Well lucky enough for you, you have rehearsals in an hour and a concert tomorrow night," he grinned, patting my shoulder.

At the mention of a concert, my heart fluttered. I may have anxiety, but I've never been nervous about performing for my fans. They are my comfort. My hope. And I can't wait to be on that stage again.

# six
## Kaili

My body is numb. My head is pounding. I took a deep breath and it felt like my body was waking up slowly. I felt a soft material covering from my belly-button down to my feet. My toes wiggled and I moved my hips, attempting to find out what I was laying down on because it definitely didn't feel like the concrete I was used to.

My head rolled from side to side and I felt a fluffy pillow under it. Pain shot through my body as I tried to bend my right arm. I opened my eyes slowly, focusing on the stinging. My breathing stopped when I saw a needle with two plastic tubes connected to it, running up to a machine and two bags full of clear liquid.

I looked around the small room and started breathing heavily. *Where am I? Why am I here? What happened to me? Am I dreaming? Surely this is just some sick dream I'm having after being beaten.*

I pulled at the tubes in my arm and an alarm sounded from behind me. I started screaming and trying to get the needle out of my arm. The door across from me swung open and a woman dressed in bright green clothes came running in.

"Shh, honey, it's okay! You're alright! Stop pulling on the tubes," she pleaded. Disregarding her, I kept pulling on the tubes and screaming, trying to wake myself up. *This can't be real.* She grabbed my hands and held them out towards her, causing me to stop moving.

My heart raced as I looked around. I let go of the tubes and tried to calm my breathing.

"What happened? Where am I?" I asked, looking at the woman. She had tears in her eyes as she watched me frantically look around for answers.

"You're in a hospital in California, sweetheart. You were beaten, honey. We almost lost you." She squeezed my hands and kept her eyes locked on mine.

"Is he here? Please don't let him hurt me."

"Who's 'he'?" She held tighter to my hands.

"The man that hurt me." I pulled back, but she wouldn't let go.

"He's in prison. It's okay. He will never hurt you again, I promise."

"What if he finds me? He's going to kill me! I don't want to die!"

"Shh. You're fine, sweetie. I'm going to need you to calm down, alright? It's okay. Just breathe, honey. You're safe now."

She sat down beside me on the bed and held my hands a little looser than before. My breathing slowly settled. I felt tears streaming down my face as the woman stared into my eyes. Her eyes were filled with tears and she sighed. She smiled at me and I took my hands from her grasps, looking at my scarred wrists.

Tears continued to run down my face and I felt the woman's eyes staring at mine. I sniffled and tried to contain my sobs. The woman moved to the chair on the right side of my bed and held my hand again. I took deep breaths and clinched my eyes shut before opening them again.

"What's your name?" She asked.

"Kaili," I answered quietly.

"I'm Sam. I'm one of your nurses."

Her face held a warm smile. I unintentionally eased into her touch, but tried to stay far from her just in case this was a dream or joke of some sort.

"How long have I been here?" I felt uneasy. I wanted to believe everything she was saying. I wanted to believe it so bad. But this was just too good to be true.

"Since yesterday afternoon. It's a quarter to three in the afternoon now," she held my hand with one hand and rubbed circles on the top of it with the other.

"How old were you when you were taken, sweetie?" Her voice reminded me of Mom. I knew if Mom were here, she'd comfort me. But she's not.

"Ten."

Sam sighed and looked down at the floor, shutting her eyes and shaking her head. I saw a tear fall from her eye and I was confused. *Why does she care?* I squeezed her hand and she looked up at me. She shook her head and smiled sweetly. I wiped my face and looked down at my legs.

I pulled the sheet off of me and looked at my bare skin. I was covered in bruises and scrapes and my clothes were gone. The only thing on my body was an ugly blue dress-thing.

"He really got me good this time, huh?" I asked timidly, looking at Sam. She nodded and looked at my legs.

"How are you so calm about this? Have you been beaten like this before?" She asked me, running a finger under her eyes to wipe her tears away.

"When he's drunk, he beats me and rapes me. This is the worst it's been, though," I tried to shake the scary memories away. She shook her head and stood up.

She pulled some pillows and blankets out of a small closet and shut the door.

"What day is it?" I asked her.

"October sixth," she smiled, looking at the calendar. She placed the blankets at my feet and put the pillows on both sides of me so my arms were propped up more comfortably. I managed to smile and thank her quietly.

"Yesterday was my eighteenth birthday," I whispered. Sam turned and smiled down at me.

"Well happy birthday Miss Kaili. I'd say getting rescued is a pretty good birthday present, huh?" She beamed. I nodded and took a deep breath, wincing at the pain in my back.

"I'll say," I grinned.

There was a black band around my upper arm that I hadn't seen before, but I didn't ask what it was. I figured it was pointless to ask what it was if I wasn't going to understand the words she'd tell me anyway.

A tall man with grey hair knocked on the open door and offered me a warm smile before speaking.

"Hello sweetie, I'm one of your doctors. My name is David Richards but you can call me Doctor Richards. How are you feeling?" He spoke calmly.

"My whole body hurts," I admitted.

Doctor Richards wrote down some stuff on the clipboard at the end of my bed and frowned.

"So your name is Kaili? Well, Kaili, you'll probably be pretty sore for a while. Your body is extremely malnourished and you were beaten pretty heavily. Do you remember anything from yesterday?"

He pushed a button on the screen thing beside my bed and the black band around my arm filled up with something. I'm assuming it's air, but what do I know?

"I remember screaming when he came down to the basement and swinging a baseball bat at him. I think he hit me and I blacked out, but I can't remember anything else." I scrunched my nose as the band squeezed my arm. He nodded and read some numbers off a screen for Sam to write down.

"Well your concussion is slowly decreasing and your blood pressure is going back to normal. The cuts on your legs will scar, but they should heal completely within the next few months. The gash on your back is still pretty bad and all the nerve tissue in that area is completely destroyed, so you shouldn't feel any pain from it. But there is something I wanted to discuss with you. Would you like for Mrs. Edwards to stay in here with us or do you want her to leave for a minute?"

He sat down in the chair beside my bed and kept his eyes locked with mine. I looked up at Sam and she smiled at me. I've only known her for a few minutes but I feel comfort in her presence.

"I want her to stay," I whispered. Doctor Richards nodded and got up to shut the door. He sat down in the chair again and Sam sat at the foot of my bed.

"When you came in yesterday, you were unconscious but still breathing. One of the officers who came in with you told our staff that you had been kidnapped some time ago and it looked like you had been in that basement for a really long time. I'm sure that was very traumatizing for you and I hope the best for you. Now with that being said, there's a slight chance that you've developed what they call Stockholm Syndrome. Do you know what that is?" He spoke slowly, which was appreciated considering I didn't know half the words he had used. I shook my head.

"Stockholm Syndrome is when someone has a physical or emotional attraction to the person who's kidnapped them or held them hostage. Have you ever felt like that towards your kidnapper?" He asked and I shook my head as fast as I could.

"Well I ask this because while we were testing all of your vitals and such, we discovered that you're pregnant. Were you aware of this already?"

*Pregnant? How?* Well, I know *how*, but what I don't know is what I am supposed to do about it. I can't take care of a baby. I can't even take care of myself. I shook my head and Sam laid a hand on my leg.

"No, I... He..." I couldn't stop myself from crying as I tried to explain what happened.

"He raped her. Many times," Sam spoke up and Doctor Richards took a deep breath.

"As your doctor, I am not authorized to inform the police about this unless you give your consent, but I hope you will alert them of this. Whether you choose to keep the baby or not, the police need to know what has happened."

He stood up while he spoke and wrote down a few things on the clipboard Sam handed him. All I could do was nod because I was afraid that if I spoke, I'd start crying again. Sam thanked him and he left the room, clicking the door shut behind him.

She walked to the foot of my bed and looked at a different clip board on the wall. She read over all of the words and looked back at me a few times with confusion swimming in her eyes.

"What's your last name, sweetie?" she asked, looking back at the paper.

"Taylor," I replied. She nodded and I looked over my legs one last time before covering them again. I never really noticed how bad they looked until now. It must be the lighting in here or something.

"Do you have a brother named Mark?" She asked casually and I froze.

*Mark.*

She knows *Mark.*

She looked at me and I felt my heart racing. I nodded slowly at her and her face lit up.

"Let me go make a few phone calls, sweetie. I'll be back in a bit," she beamed. I was still shocked from hearing the name. She practically skipped out of my room and into the hall way.

I sat confused in my bed for a good two minutes before finally snapping out of my trance. I saw a television remote on the bedside table. I reached for it and grabbed it before turning on the television that was in front of my bed. I looked again at the table, seeing Dad's military tag necklace. I clinched it in my small hand and kissed it, looking up at the ceiling.

"Thank you, God," I spoke, putting the necklace back around my neck and down the front of my gown.

I flipped through several channels on the television before settling on a news channel. I watched contently as the guy talked enthusiastically about the weather. I used to watch the weather with Dad and we would always make fun of the weather men's hair and goofy suits. I smiled to myself at the thought before the news went on to media news.

"New coming teen star Bradley Michaels battles it out for top spot on Billboard charts. His only competition? World-wide super star Mark Taylor," a fancy clothed woman spoke in a nasally voice. My eyes darted to the television at the mention of the name. There's no way she's talking about *my* Mark Taylor. No way.

I turned the volume up and watched as the makeup-coated woman blabbed on. Sure enough, a photo of my brother popped up on the screen. He looked much older than the last time I saw him, which was to be expected. It has been eight years, of course. He's bigger, obviously, but still the same.

"Mark has yet to comment on the situation, but I feel a battle coming on! Go on Twitter right now and tell us what you think! Make sure to mention our page @SlamNews and use the hashtag #MarkvsBradley. This is Tonya Marshall for Slam News," she signed off. I turned the volume down as a commercial for a cruise played and sat back, stunned. *My brother is an international pop star.*

*My brother.*
*Mark.*

# seven
## Lia

Mark stood on stage with his backup dancers, listening to the head choreographer telling him to run through his last song one more time. He has a concert here tomorrow night and needs the extra rehearsal.

"Come on, man. One more time. You have to nail this," the choreographer barked, clearly annoyed with the lack of enthusiasm coming from Mark.

He looked exhausted. Oh well, that's show business. He is going to have to get used to this pressure if he plans on staying in this industry much longer. Poor guy doesn't have much fight left in him. I believe in this kid more than anyone else, but he's missing something. It's like he's losing his inspiration. His drive. His spunk. Almost like he's giving up more and more every day.

I felt my phone vibrate in my hand and I looked down at it. It was an unknown number attempting to call me. I was always skeptical about these kinds of calls. Here recently, Mark's fans have found my number and have called me from restricted numbers. I decided to answer just to get rid of the little brats.

"Lia Martin Management, this is Lia. How may I help you?"

"Hi Lia, this is Samantha Edwards. I'm a nurse at the Los Angeles General Hospital and I am looking for a mister Mark Taylor. Is he available?" *Yeah, okay.*

"This is his manager. He's busy at the moment. What's going on?" I checked my watch and scrunched my nose at how early in the afternoon it was.

"We have his sister, Kaili."

My eyes widened and my jaw dropped as I looked over at Mark who was dancing with a bored look on his face. My left hand covered my mouth as I struggled to find words to say to the woman on the other end of the line.

"Ma'am? Are you still there?" Her voice made me jump and nearly drop my phone.

"Yes. Yes I'm still here. Are you… Are you sure it's Kaili?" I replied quickly.

"Yes ma'am it's her. She told us her name and we pulled up her old medical DNA records to verify. She's Kaili Marie Taylor. Clear as day."

This is most definitely *not* a prank call.

I waved towards Tanner and he looked at me confused. He jogged towards me and I handed him the phone once he approached the end of the stage.

"Hello?" He spoke into the phone. My heart was pounding and I tried to get Mark's attention, which was very difficult considering my speechlessness.

Tanner's jaw dropped just like mine and a massive smile spread across his face.

"Okay thank you so much. I'll let Mark know," he beamed before hanging up the phone and handing it back to me.

"Mark!" I finally got the word out.

"What?" He complained, still unconsciously going through dance moves.

All it took was me saying "Kaili" for him to stop moving and look at me.

"What about Kaili?" He demanded, worry written all over him. I felt a tear falling down my cheek and wiped it away.

"She's alive. She's in the hospital down the street," I attempted to contain my joyful sobbing. His eyes widened and he looked as if he was going to pass out.

"What?" He gasped, stepping closer to the end of the stage where I stood on the floor. I nodded and sniffled.

"They found her. She's alive," I stammered. Mark stood, biting his lip and holding in his emotions.

"Wha… How?"

"I don't know, Mark, but she's alive."

He clinched his eyes shut and shook his head, covering his eyes.

"Don't play with me, Lia," he hissed, his voice muffled by his hands on his face. Tanner looked at me accusingly.

"You know me better than that. I'd never joke around about this. They found your sister, Mark. SHE IS ALIVE," I yelled at him to try and get the point across and he sat down on the edge of the stage.

Tanner dropped down beside him and grabbed his shoulder.

"I told you so. Always trust the hunch." Tanner shook his shoulder and Mark looked up at him. He gave his back a gentle slap.

"Come on, bud. Let's go get your sister," he proclaimed and the crew erupted in a fit of cheers and happy cries. My makeup was surely ruined, but I didn't care. Mark turned and looked at his best friend before nodding.

I watched as Mark enveloped his friend in a big hug before turning towards me. They both hopped off the stage and Mark stood in front of me. Without a word, he pulled me into his arms and cried on my shoulder.

"Can we go? Please?" Mark begged, tears still falling from his eyes. I nodded.

"I'll drive," I suggested. The boys followed me out of the stadium as the crew continued to set up the last minute things for the concert.

"Are you sure they have the right person? It could be a mistake." Mark grew nervous as he climbed into my car.

"It's her. I swear," I promised confidently.

"On your job?"

"On my *life*."

"How did they find her?" He asked, still stunned with the news. *Who wouldn't be?*

"I don't know. I'm sure she'll tell you everything when she sees you," I told him, pulling on to the street. He slumped back in his seat and I looked in the mirror at Tanner who shrugged his shoulders at me.

# eight
## Lia

We pulled into the hospital parking lot and parked and none of us seemed to want to make the first move to get out.

"This sounds crazy, but I'm afraid to see her," Mark expressed, looking down and tapping on his knees with his fingers.

"Why?" Tanner questioned him before I could. He looked up at me for a second and his eyes were red from crying. He wiped under his nose before dropping his head down again.

"I don't know if I want to know what happened to her. I don't know if I can take it. That's my baby sister." He kept his eyes on his knees and fiddled with his thumbs. Tanner cleared his throat and turned to him.

"Mark, listen to me. No matter what happened to her, she's still your sister. She's the only family you have left. Your parents and your grandparents are all dead. Sure Lia and I and the crew are like family, but Kaili's the real deal. She's your flesh and blood. And she needs you now more than ever. It's going to be hard for both of you. She's been in God only knows what kind of place for the past eight years and she's all you've been talking about since I met you and now you're saying you don't know if you can handle seeing her? No offense, man, but that's horrible. Yeah, she's probably pretty banged up and stuff but she's *alive*. She's still breathing and that's all that matters at this point."

Tanner's little outburst caught all three of us off guard. I don't think he knew he had it in him to come at Mark like that.

"I know. I'm sorry," Mark uttered. Tanner shook his head and unbuckled his seatbelt.

"Just bear with me here, guys. I'm scared," Mark continued.

"We know you are, but I can guarantee you she's just as afraid as you are. More than likely a lot more afraid than you. She's in a strange place filled with strange people. Imagine how she feels." I unbuckled my seatbelt and had one foot out of the door when I spoke. Mark and Tanner both glanced at me and climbed out of the car.

I knew there would be a lot of press about this. I just hoped we could get away with it for a while until everything settles down.

Mark rubbed his hands together and followed a few feet behind me. When we walked inside, a security officer locked the doors and watched the windows for photographers and unruly fans that might find out about Mark being here.

I walked up to the receptionist and she was typing away at her computer.

"Excuse me," I spoke politely. She kept her eyes on the computer and stuck her hand up, silencing me. I raised an eyebrow as she chewed her gum obnoxiously.

"Excuse me," I asserted.

"Can't you see I'm busy?" The troll nagged, twirling an ink pen in her fingers. Her eyes looked up at me over the monitor and she pushed her glasses back up the bridge of her nose. *If only I could get away with shoving them up it.*

I waved my hand behind me to tell the boys to stay quiet. *She's pissed off the wrong woman.* I put my hands on the desk counter and clicked my tongue to try and settle myself. I opened and closed my mouth a few times, thinking of the right thing to say to get her to do her job. Looking around at the front of her desk, I noticed a name plate. Violetta. *How fancy.*

"Alright, sweet pea. My name is Lia Martin and I'm here with Mark Taylor to see his sister who was taken from his family eight years ago. I have been running on less than three hours of sleep for the past nine months, I have managed several worldwide stadium tours all by myself and, quite frankly, I don't have time for you to be 'too busy' twiddling your thumbs. Now unless you want me to march through those doors and find her myself, I suggest you swallow that gum, put down that pen, and call someone to come get us. Have I made myself clear, Violetta?" I tapped my fingernail on her desk and she looked up with wide eyes.

Tanner was laughing quietly and I kept my eyes locked on Violetta as she fumbled with the phone.

"Yes ma'am. I'm very sorry ma'am," she told me, straightening up in her chair. I turned and zeroed in on the boys and noticed the security guard was watching me. He backed up a step when I looked at him, which was quite amusing.

I looked back to Violetta and she had the phone pressed to her ear.

"Yes, I have Mark Taylor waiting in the lobby... His sister... Yes... Okay, thank you," she rushed into the receiver. She hung up and cleared her throat.

"Would you like to have a seat and wait for them to tell her you're here?" Her voice was much nicer and I rolled my eyes.

Flipping her off didn't seem like an appropriate reply, so I mumbled a sharp, "Yeah, whatever."

I turned and Mark was bouncing on his toes. The phone rang behind us and Violetta picked it up.

"Breathe, dude," I whispered to Mark. He took a deep breath and looked at the floor.

"Mister Taylor? She's coming down here to meet with you right now." Violetta stood up as she smiled flirtatiously at Mark.

"See? It's really easy to do your job, isn't it?" I sassed. Tanner stepped up behind me.

"Okay, I think someone needs to calm down." He grabbed my shoulders and pulled me away and I huffed at him.

My phone rang in my pocket and I pulled it out to answer it.

"Mark, its James." I showed him the ringing phone and he shook his head.

"I'll call him later," he blew me off, bouncing on his toes. The ringing stopped and I sighed.

"You realize you still have half a tour to finish, right? You can't just blow off the head of your record label. He's expecting a lot from you this tour. It's your biggest one yet," I explained to him. I adjusted my suit jacket and ran my hands over my slick pulled-back hair.

"Lia, I'm about to see my sister for the first time in a really long time. Can you just not talk to me about the tour right now? I have way too much going on in my mind. Just, not now."

He has never blown up on me like that. He sounds stressed. He's always stressed, but this was a different kind of stressed. I don't blame him, though. I just wish he'd realize he still has responsibilities outside of this hospital.

I'm sure Kaili will be with us the remainder of the tour, but I hope Mark doesn't lose focus. He's in his prime and I'd hate for him to miss his opportunity to become bigger and better.

He fixed his hat and looked at Tanner. Neither one of them made a sound. I thought back to the beginning of Mark's career and how I had become a mother figure for him. He had lost everyone. I can't imagine what that was like for him, so I tried my best to be there for him. I remember when I first met him.

At the time, I was just a management intern for Lakin Records. He came in with Will Lakin and his son, Tanner. Mr. Lakin owns the company and building, so everyone was pretty receptive to whatever he said. Tanner was still pretty depressed at that time. He kept his head down and his hood up and refused to speak. The only time he looked up was when I asked a question about Mark's sister. I remember telling the team that we shouldn't use her as a marketing tool. Tanner looked up and smiled at me, like he knew I wasn't as heartless as the rest of the executives.

After hearing Mark's personal life, they wanted him to sing. When he sang, the room was hypnotized. He sang a song his mom sang to him when he was little; "I Love You Because" by Johnny Cash. I also remember how quick Mr. Lakin assigned me to Mark's career. He told me I could make or break him, which was a huge weight on my shoulders. I was terrified, of course, but very hopeful.

I smiled at the memory and shook my head, thinking about how much has changed since that day. I looked back to Mark and he had his head ducked, looking at the floor. He was bobbing his head and moving his feet like he does when going through dance steps in his head. *He's nervous.* In that brief moment, I made a conscious decision to focus on him as a person rather than him as a performer. He needs to take care of his sister.

"Alright, bud. We all know what's going to come out of this. You will be your sister's legal guardian until she's 100 percent capable of doing things on her own. Tanner and I will help and I'm sure other people will too. She's going to need a new social security number, dental insurance, health insurance, and all that good stuff. She'll also need a tutor to travel with us to get her caught up and out of school. That will take a long time, but she needs that.

"She's going to need a bunch of things to help her get used to this lifestyle of yours. She'll need her own cell phone and all new clothes. She'll need a bunch of personal things and her own bedroom in your house in Atlanta when we go back. She will also need a bunk in your tour bus. I'm sure she'll need a therapist at some point, too. I can find the best one in the country and hire them to work with her.

"Now, I'm sure you both will have a lot of questions for each other, but there's going to be things she won't tell you for a long time. Hell, she might not tell you at all. But do not pressure her. That will only make her afraid of you and you don't want that, do you?"

I spoke to Mark as quietly as I could and he kept his head ducked. When he finally looked up at me, he had tears in his eyes. I sighed and frowned at him.

"Do you think she'll be afraid of me anyway?" He whispered. I shrugged my shoulders and he dropped his head again with a sigh.

"I don't know. I bet not, but I don't know what she's been through," I started.

"If anything, she'll look to you for protection. You're the only family she has left and she's going to cling to you," Tanner finished my thought for me and I nodded my head at him.

# nine
## Kaili

I took another bite of my cherry flavored gelatin as my eyes drifted back to the television. It was an old game show my mother and I used to watch. I couldn't help but wonder about my family; where they were, what they were doing now, if they forgot about me.

I felt a tear run down my cheek and I took a deep breath. I placed the now-empty gelatin cup on my bedside table and rubbed my face. I looked down at the pajama's Sam had brought me and smiled. She had bought me a pair of red plaid pajama pants and a black tee-shirt to wear instead of the "hideous tablecloth", she called it. *God bless that woman. She's amazing.* I often wondered why she cared, but I didn't dare question her intentions.

I heard a knock on my door and I flinched out of habit.

"Come in," I stammered weakly. The door opened slowly and Sam came in with a big smile on her face. She sat down at the foot of my bed and looked at me. She placed her hand on my leg and her tongue darted out to wet her lips before she smashed them together. I was slightly confused, yet waited patiently for her to speak.

"Your brother is coming to see you," she grinned, her voice barely over a whisper. My heart seemed to stop completely.

*How?*

*How did he find me?*

*Where is he?*

I couldn't speak. It was like my brain couldn't process the words.

"I found his manager and called her. Mark is on his way here, now." She stood and I looked up at her. She smiled down at me and started to walk out of the room.

"Sam?" I finally spoke. It came out as more of a cry than I had planned. So many thoughts ran through my mind, but they were a jumbled mess to say the least.

"Yeah, sweetie?" She turned and looked back at me.

"Thank you. For everything," I croaked.

"You're more than welcome."

"When can I leave?"

"Late tonight is when you are scheduled to be released, but we're taking you off of the heavy medication soon so you won't be as drowsy anymore. The police have scheduled a day next week for you to be questioned and stuff. But besides that, you're out of here. You're free."

Free. I haven't heard that word in a long time. I haven't felt freedom in such a long time. I nodded and she smiled down at me once more.

"Come on, honey. Let's get you up and moving," she declared, holding her hand out towards

54

me. I looked down at my IV and looked back up at her.

"Oh, right. One second," she giggled, walking out of the room. I watched as she came back in with another nurse. The other nurse introduced herself as Diana and she took the needle out of my arm while Sam held my hand. I thanked them both before Diana left the room.

Doctor Richards appeared in the doorway with a smile on his face. It wasn't one of those fake smiles the other nurses had given me. It was genuine, like Sam's.

"The receptionist downstairs called. Mark is in the lobby waiting for you. Do you want us to send him up or do you want to meet him down there?" He asked. I suggested "down there," the same time Sam said "send him up". She snorted and shook her head, but smiled and helped me stand up anyway.

We carefully made our way into the elevator, her right arm around my waist and my left over her shoulder. I felt my legs becoming weak as the elevator moved.

"Are you nervous?" She asked me, looking at the elevator monitor that told us what floor level we were passing. I nodded. I was terrified and excited all at the same time.

My thoughts left as the elevator doors slid open, revealing the lobby to us. With the help of Sam, I hobbled out and scanned the room for my brother. Sam searched around and her hand tightened around my waist as she stopped moving.

I followed her eyes and saw a tall boy with his back towards me, talking to another much taller boy and a woman with pretty blonde hair. He wore dark jeans and a blue sweatshirt. He had a dark grey snapback hat on his head and I knew who it was instantly.

My breath hitched in my throat and I struggled to find the words. Sam held tighter to me so I wouldn't fall over.

"Mark?" I whispered. The boy turned and looked in my eyes. His eyes drifted everywhere on my body, looking at all of my bruises and wounds from a distance. I touched Sam's wrist and she let go of me, backing away slowly to make sure I was capable of standing on my own.

I felt a tear fall from my eye as Mark took a step closer. He's much taller than me and his facial features are more defined. He has Dad's brown eyes and Mom's nose. He has short black hair and dimples when he bit his lip.

"Kaili?" He finally croaked out. It seemed to be more of a self-realization for him than a question. I nodded my head and watched as he took another step closer to me before pulling me into a loving embrace. I wrapped my arms around his neck, my face nuzzled in his chest, and held him as close as possible as we both cried. I finally had him back and I couldn't stop crying.

My legs were weak. Heck, my whole body was weak. He didn't seem to notice as he held me. His arms felt familiar and warm. He held the back of my head with one hand and the other stayed on my back. I felt like I was hugging my dad again. I felt completely safe standing in his arms. I never knew how much I had taken hugs for granted until this moment.

"I'm so sorry we couldn't find you. I'm so sorry, Kaili," he cried into my hair. I shook my head, unable to speak for a little while.

We hugged for what seemed like hours but, in all reality, it was no more than a minute. After releasing him from my arms, I wiped my face with my hands. I sniffled and took a deep breath. Mark did the same and looked over at the two people behind him. He waved for them to come forward, both with huge smiles.

"Kaili, this is my best friend Tanner and my manager Lia," he pointed to them as he stated their names.

I smiled at them and heard Sam shift on her feet behind me.

"This is one of my nurses, Sam," I smiled at her as she stepped forward.

"Ahh, yes. I believe I spoke on the phone with you," Lia stated, sticking her hand out towards Sam. She smiled before shaking her hand and I couldn't stop staring at my brother. Sam and Lia chatted and I felt Tanner's eyes on me. I smiled nervously at him and he stepped towards me.

"I can't believe someone finally found you. You are literally all Mark talks about," he mentioned, patting my brother on the back. Mark smiled at him and I sighed. It was a happy sigh, needless to say.

We stood in the lobby chatting for a while and I felt tired. I became light headed and put my hand on

Mark's shoulder. He flinched before looking at me with deep concern.

"You okay, Sis?" He asked. Sis. I missed hearing that word. I nodded and steadied myself before letting go of him.

"Um, can we go back to my room? I'm a little dizzy," I looked at Sam. She nodded and started to walk towards me to help me but Mark stopped her.

"I got it," he smiled and put his arm around my waist. I smiled at my brother and placed my arm over his shoulder. We started to walk and everyone followed behind us.

"I have so many questions," Mark whispered as we walked towards the elevator. I nodded at him in agreement.

"Me too, but can we talk later? Alone?" I asked, not wanting to explain everything to two other total strangers. He nodded in agreement and we got in the elevator.

The ride up to the tenth floor was silent. Nobody spoke or seemed to move. Getting out of the elevator, Lia spoke only to ask where my room was. When we got back to my room, she and Tanner looked afraid to follow us in.

"It's fine. You can come in," I assured them. They hesitantly stepped into my small room and sat down in chairs across from my bed. Mark helped me sit down and get situated in my bed before sitting by my feet. He looked around the small room before his eyes met mine again. He looked scared and heartbroken. I didn't want to ask why, especially not in front of his friends.

After a few minutes of meaningless chatter about things I didn't understand, Mark looked at Tanner and tilted his head towards the door. He caught the hint and stood up.

"Hey Lia, I'm getting pretty tired. Can we go back to the hotel or something?" He asked. Lia agreed and stood before coming to my side.

"It was so nice to finally meet you, sweetheart," she commented, squeezing my hand in hers. I smiled and nodded and she patted Mark on his shoulder. Lia stepped out and closed the door behind her, leaving Tanner to talk to Mark and I alone.

"We'll come back later, okay?" Tanner spoke to me and my brother. Mark smiled and nodded. Tanner patted his shoulder and they did a strange handshake.

"You'll be out tonight, right?" This time his question was directed at me. I smiled up at him and nodded my head. Tanner smiled before giving Mark one last look and leaving my small room.

As the large wooden door clicked shut, I felt my heart pounding. I was afraid to ask too many questions, but I wanted to know.

"Where are Mom and Dad?" I finally asked.

Mark looked down at the floor and shook his head. He let out a shaky breath and licked his lips.

"I knew you were gonna ask that. They, umm, they both passed away. About eight years ago, actually. Dad was killed in a fighter jet crash and Mom committed suicide soon after," he revealed, tears falling from his eyes.

My heart shattered. I couldn't believe it. *They're gone*. I took a deep breath and looked down at my hands. Tears landed on my wrists as I let the news about my parents sink in. Mark put his arm around me and held me as the tears continued to fall.

"I lived with Grandma and Grandpa till I turned eighteen, then I moved to Los Angeles. I lived on the streets for a while, occasionally breaking into empty hotel rooms. I played my guitar and sang on the sidewalks for money.

"That's when I met Tanner. He saw me playing one day and stuck around for a while before introducing himself. Turns out his father owns this big record company in LA and knew they were looking for a fresh sound. Like, he isn't the head of the label. He literally owns the entire building. Anyway, they let me live with them and my career literally went sky-high from there," Mark told me the story about his rise to fame.

I was thankful that he changed the subject. I had done enough crying for the day. I looked down at my swollen stomach and clinched my eyes shut. Mark noticed my painful expression and looked at me with worry.

"What's wrong? Do I need to call someone?" He asked. I shook my head and rested my hand on my stomach.

"You don't have to tell me, ya know," he spoke quietly. He tried to comfort me by touching my arm and I shook my head again. Whether I wanted to tell him or not, he needed to know.

# ten
## Mark

I studied Kaili's face and waited for her to speak. I was curious to know what the sick man did to her, but at the same time I wasn't sure if I wanted to know. I cared too much about my sister to make her speak about her past experiences so soon. She seemed unashamed to tell me, and I was relieved that she still trusted me so much.

I haven't seen her in eight years. Eight long years. I had so many questions. What happened to her at first? Did he touch her? Did he beat her? Did he yell at her? Did he try to kill her? *What happened to my baby sister?*

My thoughts where silenced when I saw a tear streaming down her face. She sniffled and cleared her throat. Then, her voice came out shaky and unsure.

"When he first took me, he threw me in the back of his truck and I blacked out. When I woke up, he was driving down a highway and I was scared. I tried to get other people's attention, but he pointed a gun at me and I just laid down in the truck. I remember shaking and just praying that Dad would find me.

"When he stopped the truck, we were in front of an old house. He grabbed me by my hair and held a knife to my throat. He said so many bad things to me, and I don't remember what he said exactly, but I know he called me worthless and a piece of trash or something like that. He tried to cut my throat, but I fought back. That's when he beat me and threw me into the basement.

"He would come down in the basement just to beat me and try to rape me. He, uhh, he raped me about four years ago for the first time and I felt broken. It was horrible. I found a rusty razor blade and started cutting my arms and legs. I guess I did it just to feel pain from myself instead of the pain from him. They would bleed for a while, but I never felt better. I tried so hard to get out of there. I tried breaking the door down or busting the window, but he always caught me and beat me. I tried beating him up once, but he was drunk and nearly killed me.

"That's what he would do. He'd go and get drunk and beat me and I'd try to get out but I never could. I even tried to kill myself just to get it over with. I knew I'd eventually die down there, but I guess God had other plans."

As she spoke, I felt my blood pressure rising. How could someone be so cruel to her? What did Kaili ever do to him? Not a damn thing. Why? Why did he have to take my sister? Why did he have to destroy my family? Why the hell is that sick man still breathing?

As if she heard my thoughts, Kaili put her hand on my wrist. I was furious, and she knew it. I looked in her eyes and saw nothing but fear. I hated that. I hated seeing my sister so scared. I was supposed to protect her. I was supposed to be there for her when things went wrong. But I couldn't because of a man wanting a toy.

"How did you end up here?" I finally asked her, trying my best not to go insane and find the man who inflicted all this pain and suffering onto her. She furrowed her eyebrows and looked down, thinking. She scrunched her nose as she thought and I couldn't help but chuckle.

"What?" She asked, looking back up at me.

"You used to do that when we were little," I giggled. She smiled and raised up her shirt slightly, showing multiple bruises and scars. I gasped and reached out to touch them but she flinched, so I backed off.

"He was drunk. And when he got drunk, he would leave the upstairs door open while he beat me. I don't know why, but that's always how I knew he was drunk. I started asking God how I could get out and all I heard was Him telling me to scream, so I did. I hit the man with a baseball bat and he kept beating me. I screamed as loud as I could and heard someone upstairs running down the steps. I was knocked out and woke up in this hospital bed this morning. Apparently, I got here last night, but I was still unconscious. Sam said they almost lost me," she explained.

I watched as a tear fell from her left eye and I tried to contain my emotions. She sniffled and wiped her face. When I looked down at her wrists, I was grieved to see that they were covered in scars. It made me sad to think that she had gotten that depressed.

She was ripped away from her family and held hostage in a basement for eight years. I would be depressed too. Hell, I would have just ended my life if

I was her. But I am so glad she wasn't strong enough to. I don't know what I would do if a police officer came to my house to tell me my sister was found dead. It would crush me.

We sat in silence for what seemed like hours before Kaili spoke.

"What now?" She questioned, playing with the end of her shirt. I studied the blanket draped across our laps and sighed. That was an excellent question that I, quite frankly, didn't know the answer to.

"Well, you still have to talk to the police and stuff. But I'm not sure about after that. I guess you're going to come and live with me," I spoke as I thought. A wide grin tugged at my lips as I looked at my sisters overwhelmed expression.

*That's it.*

Kaili is going to live with me! She will finish the tour with me and we will go from there. She can have a bunk in my tour bus and everything. Excitement swept over me and I couldn't help but wrap her in a massive hug.

"I love you, Mark," she cried into my neck. I smiled and held her tighter.

"I love you too, Sis. I'm so glad someone found you. I have my baby sister back," I confirmed to her. She sniffled and squeezed my torso tighter. Our hug was interrupted when my phone vibrated in my back pocket.

"What was that?" Kaili asked, pulling out of my arms. I looked at her confused and read the text message from Tanner saying that I needed to head back to the arena. Apparently I have another quick interview tonight. *Fantastic*.

"It's an iPhone," I replied, handing her my phone. She held it like it was precious gold. I watched her face as she studied it and couldn't help but giggle at her.

"It's like a normal phone, but a lot better," I continued. She looked at me with even more confusion.

"You really don't know about cell phones, do you?" I asked her. She looked back down at it and shook her head. My heart sunk. If she didn't know about cellphones, who knows what else she's clueless about? Probably just about everything. She looked it over once more before looking over at me again, completely amazed.

"There's only four buttons on this thing! How does it work? How do you use it?" She shot questions at me like a machine gun. I grabbed it out of her hands and unlocked it, showing her what I was doing.

We both jumped when a knock came to the door. I looked at my sister before standing to go answer it. I opened it to find a man in a postal service uniform.

"Is this Kaili Taylor's room?" He asked. He seemed nervous. I nodded and crossed my arms over my chest like I've watched my body guards do countless times. I almost smiled at the thought.

"Yeah, I'm her brother," I answered. The man extended his hand to me.

"I'm Andrew."

Despite having no idea who this 'Andrew' guy is, I still shook his hand. He gave off a nice guy kind of vibe, but I was still hesitant.

"I… I found her," he silenced my thoughts. My heart dropped to the floor and I couldn't help but stare at him.

"I just wanted to make sure she was okay," he continued.

"Mark? Who is it?" Kaili called from behind me. Andrew patted my arm once before stepping around me and entering the room. I took a deep breath and caught the tear that was running down my face before closing the door and turning around. He sat down in the chair beside her and she seemed uneasy.

"Hi. I'm Andrew. I was the one who found you yesterday," he told her. Her face flushed and she began to sob before wrapping her arms around the man.

My body tensed. *He saved her. Why am I threatened by him?* I guess my brotherly instincts kicked into overdrive when I saw her for the first time earlier. I couldn't help but think of what would have happened if he wasn't there.

"I was at the house next door delivering mail when the guy showed up and I heard screams. I called 911 but I didn't think they'd get there quick enough, so I ran in and found a baseball bat. Part of it is still kind of blurry to me but I remember running downstairs and hitting him with it and he passed out and you were on the floor. I don't know what came over me, but I'm glad you're alright," he spoke once they were done crying.

"Thank you," I finally choked out. He looked up at me and nodded. Kaili rubbed her eyes and I smiled at her. My sister is so broken, yet so trusting and compassionate. I know my fans will love her.

Andrew didn't stick around too long. He gave us his cell phone number to keep just in case Kaili needed a witness for court. I wanted to properly thank the man, but I couldn't find the right words. A simple "thank you" was all I could muster up but it seemed to be enough for him.

Kaili and I didn't talk much after that. I think we were both still shook up from seeing each other again. I know I was. I studied every bruise and scar I could see and controlled all the anger I felt towards the sick bastard the best I could.

"What's that?" Kaili's voice was timid and raspy. I wonder if she'll ever be the same as she was before she was taken. I doubt it. Being kidnapped is bad enough, but going through everything she's gone through in the past eight years is incomprehensible.

She was looking at my wrist when I realized that she had asked me a question.

"Hmm?" I hummed. She pointed at my tattoo and I lifted my arm closer to her.

"Well everyone thinks it an infinity symbol, but it's really an eight," I told her. Her forehead creased in confusion.

"That's my number," she mumbled.

*What?*

"No, that's my number. It always has been," I furrowed my eyebrows at her in confusion. Her eyes met mine and I cocked my head to the side.

"How is it your number?" I asked. She licked her busted lip and winced.

"Well Dad gave me a puppy when I was eight, Mom and Dad had been married for eight years when I was born, you're older than me by two years and eight months, and it was eight steps from the front door to the basement door. And I guess now I can say I was gone for eight years. Why is eight your number?" She opened up a gelatin cup as she spoke and scooped some out with a spoon.

"Umm, I have eight Grammys, I was eight when we moved out of Japan, and I've had eight broken bones in my lifetime. I guess I can add that you were gone for eight years to my list now, too."

I felt bad that my reasons were more pleasant than hers, but I can't change that. Just knowing that eight is just as intense for her is pretty crazy. Now the tattoo means so much more to me.

"What's a Grammy?" She asked and I sighed. It's going to be hard for her to adapt to the world today. It's evolved so much since we were kids. Although I'm sure we watched The Grammys as kids, I doubt she remembers it.

"The Grammys is an awards show. It's like the highest honor in music you can get. The actual awards are called Grammys," I explained it the best I could.

"And you have eight of them?" She raised her eyebrows.

It hadn't really set in yet that I had a Grammy let alone eight. So when she said that, I felt like a ton of bricks had been dropped on my back. It was quite a bit of pressure to say the least.

"Yeah," I answered her. She had the proudest smile on her face and it made me so happy to see her that way.

"Mark, that's amazing! That means you're really good, right?" Her cheeks were stretched into a massive smile.

"I guess so. It didn't really hit me until you said it, but I guess someone thinks I'm worthy of eight Grammys." I smiled along with her. She threw her arms around me and congratulated me over and over. It felt amazing to hear that from my baby sister.

# eleven
## Sam

Kaili's room number lit up on my computer and I stood up, grabbing the supplies I would need to check her heart rate and her wounds. I knocked on the door and heard her small voice tell me to come in.

"Hey guys, I just need to check on some stuff. How are you feeling?"

I walked in as they were breaking apart from a hug and Kaili looked up at me and smiled. I felt my heart split in two seeing this broken and traumatized girl finally getting to see her brother again. It was very touching.

"I'm okay I think. My belly still kinda hurts," she spoke with more confidence.

I nodded and strapped the blood pressure arm band on her left arm and pressed the button on the machine, making the band inflate. She breathed deeply for me as the monitor beeped a few times. Her heart rate was normal and she seemed happy about that. It has been everywhere but normal since she got here, so I imagine she has to be feeling better.

I cleaned her wounds on her legs and the gash on her back for her and told her to get some rest. Quite a few of her wounds were close to infection, but the antibiotics caught it in time. She will have to keep cleaning them when she goes home with Mark, but that shouldn't be a problem.

"Can she come to my concert tomorrow?" Mark asked me. I frowned and shook my head.

"Her body isn't quite ready for that much physical activity. She will need at least four or five days before she starts standing and walking for longer than an hour by herself. She lost a lot of blood, Mark, and she has a concussion," I stated, pulling my gloves off and throwing them into the nearby trash can.

I felt bad for them. I lost my mother when I was about thirteen, but I still had my dad and my two older sisters to keep me company. Kaili lost everything and everyone around her. Mark did too, but he rebounded and became insanely rich and famous. Although that doesn't necessarily fill the empty void of losing family, it definitely doesn't sound like such a terrible life. He had to be a man before he even knew what being a man was all about. I'm proud of them both for being so brave. They're truly incredible, and I hope for the best for them.

"I have to go back to the arena. Lia texted me and told me I have a late night interview. But I'll be back in the morning, okay?" Mark stood behind me and rubbed the back of this neck while he broke the news to Kaili.

"She's being released tonight, but if she needs to stay longer we can arrange something," I spoke up and Mark looked over at me with bright eyes.

"No no no. I'll come back right after my interview, then. I promise," he talked to Kaili and I smiled down at her. She looked like she was about to cry and I held her hand. *The poor thing*. She just got her brother back and now he has to leave.

I backed up and let Mark get to Kaili and he sat down to hug her. I pretended to look over her paperwork while they had their moment.

"I love you. I'll see you later," Mark promised her.

"I love you too," she sighed as he stood up. I smiled at the two of them and Mark hugged me, which was quite unexpected.

"Take care of my sister please," he whispered. I felt a lump rising in my throat and I nodded at the boy. Despite all the negative stuff the tabloids spew about him, he's actually a really good kid.

"I will," I assured him.

Most of the nurses on duty were standing around the desks when I left Kaili's room.

"Did you tell him?" Doctor Richards asked me.

"I can't do that. When she's ready to tell her brother she's pregnant, she will. I don't want to make it harder on her," I answered quietly.

He nodded his head and walked into a patient's room, leaving the other nurses and I to talk.

"Is she strong enough to go on tour with him? From what I've read, she has nobody else," Ashley, our nurse's assistant, asked and I shrugged.

"As long as she doesn't overdo herself, she should be fine. She might need a wheelchair or someone to walk with her for a little while. I definitely wouldn't suggest running a marathon," I tried to make light of the situation. Kaili's case was very rare for us. She isn't just a kidnapping victim being sent home.

She's being thrown into a crazy lifestyle with the only piece of family she has left.

Mark came out of Kaili's room just as I was typing up her release papers.

"Sam?" He piped up, looking nervous.

"Yeah, sweetie," I tried to figure out if he was more scared or exhausted. Seeing a family member in the hospital is exhausting enough without the added circumstances.

"Is Kaili going to be okay?" He asked and I smiled reassuringly.

"Yeah she's going to be fine. Maybe a little weak for a while, but-"

"No, I mean mentally," he interrupted me, eyes filled with deep concern. I walked around the desk counter and grabbed his hands.

"Mark, honey, she's been through a lot but she's a tough girl. You know that better than any of us. She might have some anxiety issues, but I can assure you she will be okay. All she needs right now is to wrap her head around everything and sort out her thoughts. She's been excluded from the world for eight years so she might need yours and your friend's guidance through it. One thing I know for sure is that there's nothing love can't conquer. Just be there for her the best you can and if you need anything, don't hesitate to give us a call down here."

I felt the corners of my eyes getting wet as I spoke. Mark was in tears and I wasn't far behind. I could tell me was scared to death.

"Thank you," he mouthed the words before I wrapped my arms around him.

He left the building with a security guard to keep him safe. Once he was gone, we got a phone call from the police station. Ashley answered it, but quickly handed the phone to me.

"Nurse Edwards, how may I help you?" I spoke quietly.

"Yes, this is Officer Kelly Sykes of the Los Angeles Police Department. May I ask you a few questions, Miss Edwards?" The voice on the other end was quite demanding.

"Uhh, yes ma'am. Is there something wrong?" I leaned against the desk and Ashley watched my face.

"No ma'am, but the judge handling Miss Taylor's case is requesting all access to all of her medical records from the past few days to be used in court as evidence. Now I understand that you have a doctor-to-patient confidentiality, but considering Miss Taylor just turned eighteen yesterday, she was a minor when everything happened to her. And considering that both her parents and grandparents have passed, her only blood related guardian is her brother. Is everything I'm saying to you making sense?"

I had managed to wave Doctor Richards down in the middle of Officer Kelly's speech and held the phone between our ears so he could hear everything.

"Yes ma'am. I have her doctor here beside me if you have any questions for him," I spoke into the phone.

"Hello Doctor. Is there anything major or monumental that we should know about before we see Miss Taylor's medical paperwork?"

"Just to be clear here, there's no argument on whether we have to release the paperwork to you or not? Is there not a law against releasing a minor's medical papers?" Doctor Richards waved his hand around as he spoke, although we were the only ones who could see it.

"Not if you release them to the police for court purposes. This is an unusual case and, for Miss Taylor's sake, I am authorized to obtain the records with or without hers or your consent," Officer Kelly replied. Doctor Richards furrowed his eyebrows at me and I shrugged.

"Well, the only thing on Kaili's record that should be a concern to you is the fact that she's almost three months pregnant and the only person she's seen in the last eight years is the sick bastard who kidnapped her. Put that in your records." I gasped at his harsh words and covered my mouth.

He offered me a shrug and Kaili's room on the monitor lit up, meaning she hit the 'nurse' button on her bed remote. I grabbed a cherry flavored gelatin cup out of our mini-fridge and headed to her room with a smile on my face and a spoon in my other hand. She doesn't need to know about the police calling us. Not now, anyway.

# twelve
## Kaili

Sam came in my room with a gelatin cup in hand and a big smile.

"How'd you know I wanted that?" I asked her, taking it from her outstretched hand. She shrugged and smiled, sitting in the chair beside me. I tore it open and looked at the top of it. She handed me the spoon she brought and I thanked her.

"Kaili, honey, this world is tough. I know it's nothing compared to what you went through, but it's its own kind of horrible. Does that make sense?" She messed with the hem of her shirt and watched me take a bite of the gelatin.

"Yeah. I probably won't ever be normal," I told her. Her eyes darted up at me and she shook her head.

"Don't say that. You *are* normal. You just went through a terrifying part of your life. You're going to be okay," she argued.

"Sam, I went through eight years of Hell in a basement in God knows where. That's not normal! I'm scared, Sam! I'm scared of almost everyone and everything! I can't live like this!"

I sat back shocked at what I had said and her lip quivered. I felt something cold on my leg and realized I had squeezed all the gelatin out of its cup.

She scooped it off of me with her hands and threw it in the trash along with the gloves she was wearing. She grabbed my hands and I felt tears running down my cheeks. She let go of one of my hands to wipe my tears with a napkin and I closed my eyes.

"I know you're scared. I'm scared for you, honey. Mark will help you with that. I promise you won't be alone. The fear will go away in time, sweetie, but you have to trust your brother and everyone who's trying to help you.

"Your life is going to change very quickly, Kaili. *Very* quickly. And you're going to learn so much about who you are and what the world is all about. It's going to be hard for a while, but you will be okay. You're safe, now. You're safe," she shook my hands as she cried. Tears were running down my cheeks and I sniffled.

"How about we watch a movie, yeah? My shift ends in a few minutes and I can stick around and watch a movie with you. Is that okay with you?" She asked. I sniffled again and wiped my eyes.

"Don't you want to go home?" I countered. She smiled and shrugged her shoulders at me.

"My husband can wait a few more hours. We're both off work tomorrow, anyway. It'll be fun!" She beamed.

She finished her shift and called her husband while I looked at the pictures of movie covers in the binder she gave me.

"Did you pick one?" She came back in the room a few minutes later. I went back a few pages and pointed to a picture I thought was cool looking. It was an animated movie, but I didn't care. I lost some of my childhood, anyway.

"You want to watch that one? That's my favorite!" She smiled and I scooted over in my bed so she could sit with me.

She ordered the movie on the TV somehow and sat down beside me. We watched the movie and laughed at the funny parts and cried at the sad parts. She paused the movie as the end credits started rolling and looked over at me.

"You know, you remind me of the main character a little," she smirked. I tilted my head to the side at her and she licked her lips.

"You do. You're both afraid of the world but eventually you'll find your superpower and use it to benefit others," she continued and smiled at me while she explained it. I smiled up at her and she hugged me. Her hand ran up and down my arm and I couldn't help but sigh contently.

"Granted, she went completely crazy, but we're not gonna mention that." She giggled and I laughed with her.

# thirteen
## Kaili

Sam stuck around for a while longer and told me all about her family. She had an incredible story and I'm glad she shared it with me. Another nurse came in and checked all my stuff and told me Mark had called.

"He should be here, soon. But you can't leave until ten o'clock tonight," the nurse smiled and wrote more stuff down on the clipboard Sam and Doctor Richards had used. It was already passed seven in the afternoon.

Mark came in a few minutes later with Lia and Tanner and Sam left for the night. She wrote down her phone number on a piece of paper for me to let her know how I am every once in a while. She told me I changed her life somehow, which didn't seem fair. She changed my life more than anything. I told her I would keep in touch and thanked her for everything she'd done for me.

"What time is your concert tomorrow?" I asked Mark once everyone had gotten settled in.

"I, uhh…" He started to answer me, but Lia interrupted.

"We postponed tomorrows show for later in the tour," she looked at me and I felt confused.

"Why'd you do that?" I asked him.

A knock came to the door before he could answer me and Tanner got up to answer it. Doctor Richards and a few nurses walked in and stood around my bed.

"Hey, looks like someone's having a party in here," Doctor Richards smiled. I smiled back politely and one of the younger nurses with pink cheeks kept smiling at Mark. Doctor Richards smiled down at me and raised his eyebrows.

"Well, I have some great news for you, Miss Kaili. Looks like you get to leave a few hours early! I figure there's no need to keep you till ten since your medications are already wearing off. We'll just need yours and Mark's signature on these papers and you're free to go! Well, after we get a wheelchair to roll you down to the lobby in. Company policy."

Mark and I looked at each other and I couldn't hold back my smile.

"Really? She can come with me?" Mark asked.

"Yes sir. But we need to talk about a few things first. If you guys could give us a minute," he started talking to just us, then looked around at the nurses, Lia, and Tanner. The nurses lead them out of the room and Doctor Richards closed the door behind them.

"Okay, guys. Kaili, you have suffered a great deal of trauma and neglect and it's going to take a little while for your body to bounce back. You had a minor concussion when you came in here, but who knows how many major concussions you've had in your life in that basement. So, you're going to need to take it easy for a while. That means getting a lot of rest and letting others take care of you.

"Now as far as touring goes, I wouldn't recommend it but I'm not saying you can't. You'll just have to stay backstage or even on the bus during shows. Mark, no having her come out on stage or anything like that for a while. She can't handle all of that just yet. Maybe someday she will be able to, but most definitely not now. You're going to have to have someone with her at all times. I suggest your manager and maybe a body guard. We don't want to take any chances with something like this ever happening again.

"I also suggest taking some time off work to just spend with her. I know you're a very busy guy, but this is a very serious matter. I've prescribed her some pain and anxiety medication and an extra strength aloe ointment for her open wound on her back which you can pick up at the pharmacy down on the next block. The receipt you get with those will tell you how often to take the medicines.

"The last thing I suggest you start thinking about is speaking with the police about everything that's happened. In order for that man to get exactly what he deserves, you need to tell them exactly what happened. Everything. It probably won't be easy, but it needs to be done.

"You're being thrown into a crazy life, Kaili, but I have no doubt that you'll get used to it quickly. You just have to be careful. You're young, but you're not invincible. Neither one of you are. And if you guys need anything or have any questions, don't be afraid to call us or come by."

Doctor Richards gave us his long speech, and I was thinking that I was going to wake up from this dream soon. Mark was listening intently and nodded his head when Doctor Richards finished.

"Where do we need to start?" Mark questioned, sitting up straighter.

"There's so much that needs to be done, but I suggest just going to your hotel and letting everything settle down for a few days. Then the police will tell you everything that needs to be done. Maybe your manager can go out and kind of spit ball on clothing sizes for Kaili and buy her a few things until she's up to going shopping. Her nurse Sam bought her what she's wearing, but we don't have anything else for her to take home as far as clothing goes. Just let the next few days play out and see how everyone is feeling before you make any drastic changes."

Mark and I soaked in his words and nodded at the same time.

"Thanks," I mumbled. He nodded his head and had Mark and I sign our names on the papers. I had completely forgotten how to hold a pen. Mark's signature looked so neat and practiced. I'm sure he has to sign stuff all the time with his job.

Tanner and Lia came back in once Doctor Richards left. Lia did most of the talking and I would look over at Mark every now and then. I can imagine this is pretty bad for him. He was in the middle of a tour and now he has to take a break because of me. I feel guilty even though I know I shouldn't. I should be happy to be out and with my brother, but I feel like more of a burden than anything.

# fourteen
## Kaili

It's been a week since Mark took me home. And by home, I mean his hotel room. It was far from home, but then again, what is home anymore? His house is in Georgia, which is where we are going after the tour. He told me that the tour had a two month break to do press and awards shows in Los Angeles, which didn't seem like much of a break to me.

He has spent a large amount of money on me in the last week. I'm sure it wasn't a whole lot to him, but to me it was a fortune. He's bought me clothes and other girly things. He got me a phone and a bunch of other tech-things that I don't know the name of. I didn't see the point of having it if I don't know how to use it, but it's what every teenager has, he says.

I suppose it will take me a while to get used to the idea of being out in public with him seeing as how I can't walk two feet without someone mobbing us. He says I'll get used to it, but I don't see how anyone could.

I also quickly learned that I have a ton of hair on my head. It's thick and heavy, but Natalie says it's getting healthier by the minute. Natalie is Mark's girlfriend. She's also a singer, but she works mostly on background vocals on tracks. At least that's what Mark has told me.

She's the perfect girl; tall, curvy in all the right places, flawless skin, perfect nails, and a gorgeous face. But she's so much more than that. She has a kind heart. I would know, because she's been by my side with Mark and Tanner since I got out of the hospital. She says I will get used to being out in public very soon.

She has shown me how to do a lot of basic girly things, like how to braid my hair and paint my fingernails. She showed me how to shave my legs and underarms. And she never passed judgement or seemed like she thought she was better than me when she clearly is, which is why I like her so much.

She also taught me how to use a pad for when my "period" happens. We talked about those when it was just her and I and I told her all I had in the basement was old clothes to wear until the bleeding stopped. I had assumed I was bleeding all of those times from him punching me in the stomach or something, but she told me it was natural.

I don't know why she called it a "period", though. A period is a small dot at the end of a sentence, right? From my past, I know periods are nowhere close to being as small as a dot. Apparently, periods can be really confusing and ultimately "suck the life out of you". She says the only time a period shouldn't come at all is when you're pregnant.

*Ha.*

I just hope she doesn't eventually ask why mine hasn't happened in a while. I'm not ready to tell anyone.

Mark has me staying in the hotel room with him and he got me my own bed to sleep on. It's massive and really comfortable. I miss having my own bed in my bedroom at our old house, but this is perfect. The whole room felt very home-y and comforting. I guess any room is considered comfortable compared to the basement.

We don't talk about it much, Mark and I. I think he's just as afraid to ask me about it as I am to talk about it. I'm just not ready. I don't know if I ever will be, really. That basement is like a ghost that won't quit haunting me no matter how many ghost busters I bring into the picture.

Tanner is staying in the suite in his own room, but he spends a lot of time in mine and Mark's room. He came in our room last night and handed me a dark grey sweatshirt with a white smiley face on it. It was folded up nice and neat, which was strange since I knew it hadn't been washed yet.

"It's for you to wear when you're nervous and stuff," he explained. I'm not really sure what other "stuff" he was talking about, but I thanked him and put it on anyway. It was pretty big and smelled like Tanner's body spray.

"Thanks, Tanner," I told him, tucking my hands in the sleeves and curling the ends into my hands.

"You're welcome. Maybe becoming a normal teenager will be easier for you than you think. You've already mastered the art of sweater paws," he smirked down at me and I looked at my hands.

"Are these sweater paws?" I raised my hands up and he nodded.

"Yup, you got it. I'll see you tomorrow, okay?" He spoke quickly so I waved with my sweater paws as he left the room. Mark came over to where I was sitting and fell back onto the couch. His head landed in my lap and he smiled up at me.

"Whoa, is that Tanner's hoodie?" He asked, pointing at my stomach. I looked down at the smiley face and nodded.

"He gave it to me a few minutes ago. He said it should help when I get scared," I told my brother. He furrowed his eyebrows and looked down at his hands.

"What?" I asked him. He raised up and sat beside me properly. He shook his head and picked a piece of lent off my shoulder.

"It's just that he's had that sweatshirt for as long as I can remember. It means a lot to him." His hands rested in his lap and I thought about it for a second. *Why would he give me something that means something to him? I'm just Mark's sister, after all.*

"What do you think tomorrow's gonna be like?" I already knew I'd be scared, but I was hoping Mark could give me some sort of reassurance. He pulled at his own sweatshirt sleeves and made sweater paws before answering me.

"I don't know. I think it's going to be good for you to see him. I'm not really excited to see what he looks like, though."

"Why not?" I noticed a small smile on his lips as he turned and looked at me.

"Because. I meet a crap ton of people every single day and if I meet someone who looks anything like him, I might just go all Kung-Fu Jedi master on them. Rough 'em up a bit," he joked, waving his hands out in front of him in a way I'm assuming was supposed to resemble whatever it was he said. *Kong-I Judy something.* Whatever it was, it calmed my nerves a little.

# fifteen
## Kaili

The next morning, Mark took us to eat breakfast at a small pancake place named Hank & Dolores's. The food was incredible and I'm pretty sure by the time I finished I had eaten my entire body weight in pancakes.

"Pancakes are food for the soul," Lia told me with a mouth full, a little maple syrup running down her chin. I couldn't agree more. I felt very soulful. Or maybe it was because I ate too much. Either way, I felt full.

Today's the day I face my kidnapper at the jail house. I have to be interviewed by some police officers and point out the man in a room full of "suspects". It didn't make sense, since he was arrested in the basement the day Andrew found me.

I've also learned loads of new words this week. "Marvelous" is my new favorite word. Mark, Tanner, Lia, and Natalie are marvelous. Pancakes with chocolate milk are marvelous. Being able to eat food that hasn't expired is marvelous. Suspects, on the other hand, aren't marvelous.

I'm afraid of today, to be totally honest. I don't know what to expect from this, but Mark and Tanner made a promise to me this morning. They promised to be no more than three feet away from me the entire time we're here. Mark's body guards will also be there, but they don't make me feel as safe as I do around my brother and Tanner.

"Look, man, I'm really gonna need your help in there. Kaili's nervous," I heard Mark say in the other room. I wonder if he knows I can hear him. I don't think he does.

"She's going to be in a room full of police officers, dude. She'll be fine. Plus, we promised her we would be close at all times. Just chill, alright?" Tanner assured him. What he doesn't realize is that I probably needed to hear that more than Mark did.

I heard the boys do their little handshake thing and the door slid open. They really need a quieter handshake. Theirs is obnoxious. "Obnoxious" is another word I learned this week. As in "the paparazzi are being rude and obnoxious today". That word is fun to say.

When we got to the police station, at least twenty paparazzi men and women were standing across the street. Obnoxious. Mark and Tanner put their arms over my shoulders and walked me inside the building.

Inside, we were asked to take a seat in the waiting room. Why we are in a waiting room, I have no idea. There's nobody else in here. Not even a person at the front desk.

"They should at least have a receptionist in here," Mark spoke. That must be what they're called. *Receptionists*.

"Miss Taylor?" A large man in a black uniform stood in the doorway. I made sweater paws and crossed my arms as I stood up. I looked back and Mark and Tanner were standing behind me. Mark gently nudged me to walk and I hesitantly took a few steps forward.

"Oh, uhh, we can't have anyone else in the interrogation room," the large man held his hands up towards Mark and Tanner.

"Can we stand outside the door? She doesn't want us far from her, sir," Tanner asked. The man looked down at me and the look on his face scared me. He yelled at the police officer at the other end of the hallway and asked him if it was okay if Tanner and Mark stood close to the door.

A small woman, also in a black uniform, walked up to us and made the large man leave.

"Hi sweetie. My name is Kelly Sykes, but you may call me Officer Kelly. I read your file, and I will be asking you a few questions today. Is that okay?"

She's nice. Definitely better than the large man. I nodded and she shook my hand softly. I expected a harder handshake from a cop, but it wasn't hard at all.

Mark seemed a bit more nervous than he was before for some reason.

"Shouldn't you be going by Officer Sykes, then?" He asked her. Officer Kelly smiled and shook her head.

"My boss and I have very similar last names, so the dispatchers said I could go by my first name so we don't get confused," she told him. I looked around the room and Mark stood closer to me. Officer Kelly held the door open for me and Mark squeezed my hand. When he let go, I looked up at him.

He nodded his head towards the window and said, "I'll be right there, I promise."

I stepped inside the small room and Officer Kelly closed the door behind me.

"Usually we can't have the blinds open, but your brother spoke to me on the phone earlier and requested that he be able to see you at all times while you're here. Is that correct?" She asked. *He called?* I didn't know about that but I'm glad he did.

I nodded and she pointed at the chair behind me and I sat down. I hugged my body and took a deep breath. This sweatshirt Tanner gave me last night is serving its purpose.

She sat across from me and pulled a small device out of her pocket, laying it on the table between us.

"This is an audio recorder. It will be used to record everything we say in here today, so speak as clearly as you can, okay?" She asked and I nodded my head in reply. She pressed a button and began speaking into it.

"The date is October seventeenth and the time is ten hundred hours. Officer Kelly Sykes recording the case of the kidnapping of Kaili Taylor." She looked up at me and placed it in the middle of the table.

"Please state your name and age," she demanded quietly.

My teeth let my bottom lip loose and I flicked my tongue out to wet it.

"Kaili Taylor. I'm eighteen," I spoke as calmly as I could. She nodded her head and straightened the papers in front of her.

"Now, I only have about thirty minutes to ask you all these questions, so try to keep up. At times it may get overwhelming. If at any time you feel the need to leave, let me know and we can stop. Do you have any questions before I get started?"

"What does 'overwhelming' mean?" I pulled on my sweatshirt sleeves and laid my hands in my lap.

"It means like 'too much' or 'a lot to take in'." She sounded annoyed with me already.

"Okay."

"How old were you when you were kidnapped?" I looked at the window and Tanner made a funny face at me while Mark was looking the other way. I smiled and looked back at Officer Kelly.

"Ten." My nervousness was starting to wear off and I prayed it would stay away.

"What do you remember from that day?" She started writing on a notepad and I wondered why she did that when the recorder was still on.

"We were in Nevada at a gas station and the man threw me in the back of his truck and took me."

"Who's 'we'?" She looked me in the eyes.

"My mom, my dad, and Mark." I bit the corner of my mouth and looked down at my hands.

"Okay. What else?"

"It was dark and the man was wearing a mask, so I didn't know what he looked like yet. I was knocked out in the bed of his truck and when I woke up, we were going down a highway and it was bright out. He pointed a gun at my head when I tried to wave someone down so I just laid down. When we got to his house, he tried to kill me but I fought back. Then he threw me in the basement and I'd been down there ever since."

Officer Kelly wrote down some stuff on her paper before looking at the audio recorder on the table. She let out a sigh that I'm guessing she didn't mean to let out, because she looked up at me with wide eyes before shaking her head quickly. Her face went hard again and I looked at the floor.

"Is that where that scar on your neck came from?" She pointed at my neck with her pen.

"Yes." My fingers touched the scar as I tried to forget how rough his hands were on me. *So much for my nervousness subsiding.*

"Has he ever beat you or threatened to kill you?" Her pen glided across her paper quickly as she spoke.

"Both." His voice was ringing in my ears and I tried desperately to ignore it. He kept yelling and screaming at me.

"Has he ever tried to rape or succeeded in raping you?"

I could feel his hands on me and his growl in my ear. I shook my head to rid the thoughts, but they grew more intense.

"Yes. He raped me a bunch of times."

"How old were you the first time he raped you?" She kept firing questions and I tried my best not to scream.

"Fourteen, I think." I took a deep breath and looked at the wall behind her.

"Have you had sex with anyone since the last time he raped you?" Her stare was not as comforting as it was when we first started.

"No." I ran my hands up my arms in a desperate attempt to erase the feeling of his brutal touch.

"Has he ever been intoxicated when he beat or raped you?"

"What does 'intoxicated' mean?" I hated not knowing what words meant. It made me feel stupid.

"Drunk. Could you smell alcohol on him?" She moved her hands around as she explained.

"Oh. Yes. Every time."

"When was the last time he raped you?"

I was getting nervous and dizzy. She didn't give me much time to breathe between questions and it was giving me a headache. My ears were ringing and I kept rubbing my hands over my arms.

I looked at the window and saw Mark looking in at me. He nudged Tanner, who was focused on Officer Kelly. They both looked at me with concern in their eyes and I took a deep breath. I was tired and hurting. I felt like my entire body wanted to shut down completely.

"Miss Taylor? When was the last time he raped you?" Her voice was noticeably louder.

"Can we stop?"

Officer Kelly nodded her head and wrote down a few more things on her notepad. She stood and I did the same. I tugged on the sleeves of the sweatshirt and crossed my arms. All I wanted to do was hug Mark and Tanner.

"Officer Craig will take you to the identification area. I'll see you soon, Kaili." She touched my arms and smiled at me. She bowed her head to me and walked away right as I felt a hand on the back of my arm.

I turned around and latched onto Mark and he ran his hands up and down my back. Tanner laid one hand on my shoulder and we stood in silence in the middle of the hallway. An incredibly large man walked up to us after a few moments and held his hand out to me.

"I'm Officer Craig. Officer Kelly sent me to take you to the ID room. If you would, follow me please," he introduced himself. After I shook his hand, we followed him down a few hallways before we stood in a small room in front of a glass window. Mark and Tanner stood on either side of me and I took a deep breath.

"Lights!" Officer Craig shouted; his voice startling me. Mark grabbed my hand and a bright light came on on the other side of the glass.

I gasped when I saw him. I can't remember the last time I got a good look at the man. I'm not sure if I ever really have. He's tall. He has quite a bit of arm muscle. I see some familiar tattoos on his arms and one on his exposed collarbone I hadn't seen before. I could see the letter "E", but that's all that was visible.

I remember one of the first times he raped me. He was shirtless this time, which never happened again. His hands were on my neck and he had my body pressed against the wall. His whole body was red in anger and I was terrified. Every inch of me was hurting and there was nothing I could do about it. I just had to take it and pray to God it would be over soon.

He slapped my face and held my neck tighter until I eventually passed out while he finished raping me. I never knew why he did it, but he would always drop me to the ground when it was over and leave me to either die or wake up wishing I was dead.

"How'd you like that, you little slut?" He would ask me. All I could do was cry and bring my knees to my chest.

He has more facial hair now and a pretty nasty bruise on his forehead. I must have hit him pretty hard with that baseball bat. Harder than I thought. He's in an orange jump suit with "LA Jail" written in black letters across his chest. His wrists and ankles are in cuffs and chains and his knuckles are bruised. I watched as his eyes scanned my body. It's almost like he was studying me. What he did next will forever haunt my dreams.

He smiled at me.

# sixteen
## Mark

I heard Kaili gasp and her hand tensed up. Her body shifted closer to me. She raised her free hand and pointed at the largest man on the other side of the glass.

"That's him," she whispered, taking deep breaths and shaking. Her feet were frozen in their place and I watched the officers looking back and forth between her and me.

I looked back up at the man and felt intimidated. He was tall and massively built. He had a scar on his forehead and tattoos all over his arms. His eyes were glued to my sister and I wanted to wring his neck. He smiled at her before the police took him back.

An officer popped his head into the room, but quickly retreated when he saw Kaili and I standing there. Her breathing was slow and quiet. She kept staring at the glass, not blinking. Her fingers were glued to mine and I could feel the fear radiating off of her. I hate that there's nothing I can do to make it go away.

"Kaili?" I snapped my fingers in front of her and she looked over at me. She looked absolutely horrified and my heart broke. I grabbed her and pulled her into me. Her arms wrapped around me and she finally started crying.

"Please get me out of here," she pleaded, her face still in my chest. I held her tighter and looked for Tanner who had already made his way out of the identification room with the door open behind him. He told the officers we were leaving and opened the door wider so we could get through. He and I held on to her shaking body as we lead her out of the building.

"Is she alright?" He asked once she got in the car. I shrugged my shoulders and walked around to the other door.

"I don't think so, but I hope she will be soon," I admitted.

I jumped in beside her and she leaned against me and Tanner scooted in on the other side of her.

"How'd it go?" Lia asked, looking at me from the passenger seat. I shook my head at her and Kaili leaned farther into my chest. My arms snaked protectively around her and I felt her shudder.

"Just take us back to the hotel. Please," I begged quietly. Lia gave the driver the address and I tried my best to hold the pieces of my baby sister together.

We went back to our hotel and Kaili went to take a nap in her room. Tanner seemed to be a bit shaken up about something, which wasn't like him. He's usually so calm and laid back.

"Dude, are you okay?" I watched as he flinched and looked up at me. He let out a shaky breath and shook his head.

"It's almost Allen's death anniversary," he uttered.

Allen was his baby brother who passed away a few years ago. He doesn't talk about him much because it's too hard on him. I understand that completely. His brother was only seven when he passed away from cancer. He and Tanner were best buds.

I never got the chance to meet Allen because he passed away before I met Tanner. Their dad told me that when Allen passed away, Tanner went AWOL. He shut himself out from the rest of the world and started acting differently. It was a pretty low point in Tanner's life, so we've only talked about it a handful of times.

I sat down beside him on the couch and his chin started to quiver.

"I just wish I could have been a better brother for him," he whispered, laying his face in his hands. I put my hand on his shoulder and shook him a bit.

"You were the best brother in the world for him. You helped him live a better life, even though it was short," I did my best to comfort him although I probably wasn't helping much. I only lost Kaili for eight years. Tanner lost Allen for the rest of his life.

I can't imagine how hard it is to watch your only sibling die right in front of you. Sure, Mom and Dad had both passed away, but I didn't watch it happen. I was vaguely told how it happened. Tanner had to sit and watch his little brother take his last breath.

"I gave Kaili the sweatshirt," he mumbled after a few minutes of silence.

"I saw that. I didn't think you could ever get rid of that thing. It's a huge part of you, man. Why'd you give it to her?" I asked him. I wasn't angry, just interested to know why.

He fidgeted with his hands and shrugged his shoulders.

"I don't know. It helped me through some tough times so I figured it could help her too, ya know?"

His answer made me think. I'm glad she has it, but at the same time I wish I would have thought of something like that sooner. I felt like I was failing as a big brother. I'm not as good at it as Tanner.

# seventeen
## Tanner

"NO! LET GO OF ME!"

I sat up and hit my head on the lamp beside the bed. Kaili's voice sounded off again and I jumped up and ran across the room. She kept screaming and I couldn't get her damn door open fast enough.

I got inside her room and she was asleep, flailing her arms and legs and screaming bloody murder. I've never tried to wake up someone like this. Her right fist got awfully close to my face as she swung and I grabbed her wrist. She screamed as loud as she could and I saw tears streaming down her face.

"Kaili, wake up!" I shouted, trying to hold her arms. Her face was twisted in fear and I couldn't seem to wake her.

"Help me! Mom! Dad!" She kept screaming. I had to straddle and shake her body to wake her up, careful not to hurt her. She opened her eyes and my heart broke in a thousand pieces. Her arms held my body as close to her as she could and she took deep breaths. I had her roll over so her head was laying on my chest and I felt her tears land on me.

I thought she would want more personal space after her experiences, but based on how tight her little arms are around my body, I'd say I was wrong.

"It's okay. He can't hurt you anymore, Kaili. He's gone." I couldn't help but feel guilty that I wasn't here sooner. I just wish Mark was back from recording. I'm sure she would rather have her brother here right now.

Her body was shaking. Her legs were bunched up at my thigh, which was extremely uncomfortable. Her hair was a mess and she was sweating, but her body felt frozen. I tried to move to get under the blanket with her, but she held on tighter.

"Please don't leave," she whimpered. I shook my head and cupped her face in my hands.

"I'm not going anywhere, but I'm cold," I smiled sympathetically at her. Her arms loosened around me and I resisted the urge to kiss her head. She let me get under the blanket and latched back onto me. My body molded together with her as she gripped my shirt with her fingers.

I ran my fingers through her hair and told her over and over that she is safe now. I can't imagine what kind of dream she was having, but I hope she never has it again. She fought sleep with her head on my chest and her feet wrapped around my leg. I reached for her phone on the bed side table to check the time. Two a.m.

I texted Mark telling him she had a nightmare and that I'm in the bed with her and he said he'd be back in a little while. He told me to watch out for her while he's gone, and I really hope this isn't taking it too far. Mark's my best friend and there's no way in hell I'd ever hurt him or his sister. He means too much to me, and I'm starting to think this broken girl does too.

"Do you want to tell me what you dreamed about?" I asked cautiously. She sniffled and shook her head.

"It was just like when he first took me but I couldn't scream or fight back. It's like I was frozen and he was hitting me and cutting me," she spoke through cries and I held her tighter.

"Shh. It's okay. Don't say any more. You're okay." My hands ran up and down her back and she cried harder.

"Why won't the dreams stop?" She sobbed.

"You've had these dreams before?" I asked her, shocked and deeply saddened. She held tighter to me and that was the only answer I needed. I shook my head and started rubbing her back again, not realizing I had stopped.

"I don't know but they will go away in time," I told her.

"I hope so," she whispered back.

# eighteen
## Tanner

A week has gone by now and Kaili's court date is coming up in a few days. The day after the Music Television and Movie Awards, actually. I don't understand why they waited so long to take the case to court, but I guess I don't have to understand. As long as this whole mess gets taken care of, I'll be okay.

Natalie will be working while the trial is happening, so Mark, Lia, and I will be going with her. Mark found her a great lawyer, but I highly doubt any judge would find the man not guilty after listening to Kaili talk about it.

Today, Mark and I went to meet with his stylist to get him a suit for the MTMA's.

"You need one, too," Mark pointed at me as he informed me.

"I'm not wearing a tux," I proclaimed. He shook his head and laughed at me.

"Neither am I. We gotta look our best, though."

We shopped around for a while and Mark's stylist gave us advice on what to wear. I hate shopping with Mark's stylist, mainly because his taste in clothing is so much different than mine. I'd rather be in a pair of jeans and a band tee-shirt than a dress suit.

He told me once that the fancier you dress, the more respected you are. Bull. The fancier I dress, the more uncomfortable I am. Same way with Mark.

"Why can't I just wear an old AC/DC shirt and a pair of black jeans and call it good?" I asked the stylist. He shot me a look and I chuckled. Mark threw his sunglasses at me which made me laugh harder.

"Style is the key to your inner being, Tessa," the stylist exaggerated in his obnoxious southern accent.

"It's Tanner," I shot back, confused. He looked back at me and shook his head.

"Today you're Tessa," he placed his hand on his hip.

"Why?"

"Because you're choosing to act like a spoiled little girl instead of cooperating with me."

Mark lost it. He had to sit down from laughing so hard. I, on the other hand, didn't find it as amusing. I kept my nose in my phone for the rest of the shopping trip, trying to ignore everyone.

"Hey you should text Kaili and see if she got a dress yet," Mark suggested after a while, holding a dress shirt up to his body in front of a mirror. I nodded and sent her a text.

Mark's stylist ordered him to try several outfits on before he found the perfect one. He found me a black and silver one, too, but it wasn't as cool as Mark's. Understandable, as I'm not the celebrity.

"Remember that black goes with everything, Tessa," The designer got his final jab in before we left the shop. Mark laughed all the way out the door at the nickname.

"He's an ass," I chuckled.

"But he's good at his job," he pointed out, raising his eyebrows at the paparazzi crowding around us.

"True, but he's still an ass," I retaliated. We managed to push our way through the photographers and make it to our car without cussing anyone out. The last time we were ambushed like this, we ended up on an entertainment trash show with more bleeped-out words than the clean version of any rap song.

# nineteen
## Kaili

"I think you should go with black and silver," Natalie spoke up, pointing to a bottle of black nail polish. We were in a nail salon, getting what Natalie called a "mani-pedi" for the awards show coming up. She says it's better to get them done early in the morning so they have more time to dry and you can find a dress to match. Personally, I would think getting a dress first and nails to match would be better, but what do I know?

"Just get like your toe nails black and have an ombré sort of thing on your fingernails," she continued.

I pulled on my sweatshirt sleeves and made sweater paws, which made me think of Tanner. He's so cute, but I know he's more like a protector for me than anything. Someone I can run to.

"Whatever you think," I agreed quietly.

To be honest, this place made me feel nervous. I'm not sure why. Probably because every place I go to makes me nervous. I'm very thankful for Natalie, though. She's so understanding. Well, not "understanding" because nobody understands what I went through, but she listens and tries to help. She's like a big sister when Mark can't be here for me.

I hope he marries her one day. She has been helping me so much these past few weeks. This is what having a best friend feels like, I guess. Someone who won't judge you but will do their best to make you feel welcome and loved.

"Do you like the black and silver or do you want different colors? I'm going to get silver and gold to match the dress I already bought. But black goes with everything," she explained as we stood in front of the massive wall of nail colors. I nodded and tucked some of my hair behind my ear.

She took me to get my hair done yesterday, which seemed pretty pointless in my opinion. All they did was wash it and cut it for me. They fixed it all pretty then sent me home, just to rewash it and pull it back in a hair tie. I didn't see the point in it, but Natalie said it's to show me how I'm going to have it fixed when the award show finally happens.

Natalie and I sat down in massive chairs and put our feet in a small tub of water. The water was warm and relaxing. I felt my stomach rumble a little bit and I sighed. I need to tell Mark about my baby. *Is this something you would normally tell your best friend?* She was Mark's girlfriend first, but still. She's the closest thing to having a best friend that I've got. I knew if I didn't tell her now, I'd never have the courage to tell anyone.

"Hey, can I tell you something?" I nervously asked her. She turned and looked at me, nodding.

"Of course," she smiled. I took a deep breath and tried to think of how to say it.

*'Hey, I'm pregnant!'*

*No.*

*'Remember the guy that kidnapped me? Yeah, he raped me and got me pregnant!'*

*That's not good either.*

"Uhh, well you know how you taught me how to use those one things for periods?" I started. She looked at me funny but nodded anyway. *Here we go.*

"I probably won't need those for a while." I tried to talk as quiet as possible, even though we were the only ones in the room. She still looked confused, but her eyes suddenly widened.

"Kaili, are you pregnant?" She gaped. My heart was racing and I felt my stomach turning. I nodded and closed my eyes. I felt Natalie's hand touch mine and I let out my breath. She held my hand and I finally opened my eyes.

"Is it his?" She asked. I slowly nodded my head and she sighed.

"Oh, Kaili. Does Mark know yet?" She leaned over in her seat so she could talk quieter.

"I don't know how to tell him. He's going to be so mad at me," I frowned and looked down at the bubbles coming up in the water. Natalie reached across and grabbed my hand in hers.

"Kaili, he's your brother. He won't be mad at you. He needs to know. Especially if you're very far along. You need to see a doctor. And tell the police," she encouraged me.

"I'm afraid to."

"You need to tell the police so they can prosecute him for it. You can't just let that go! Mark and I will go with you if you want. But, like, are you

110

going to keep it?" She started to get louder but quickly realized it and spoke quietly again.

"I don't know if I can." A woman in a uniform started messing with my feet and I jerked them away from her. It took a reassuring smile from her before I slowly sat my feet back in the water and let her do her job.

"You know Mark and I will help you, right? And Tanner and Lia. You're not alone here," Natalie took a sip from her coffee she bought before we got here and pointed at me.

"I know. I'm just scared," I admitted to her. I hate being scared. Fear seems to define me, and I don't know how to change it. I wish I was as brave as her, but I'm not. Maybe someday I will be, but obviously not today.

"I would be too if I'm being completely honest. I'd be terrified. But it's going to be okay. We won't let you do this alone. We're all in this together, alright?" She smiled over at me and patted my hand as another woman started messing with her feet.

I watched the woman in front of me as she worked quietly. I wonder if anyone ever talks to her while she's working. Or if anyone has ever paid for her to have a mani-pedi.

"I don't want Mark's fans to hate me. This makes my situation even worse," I told Natalie, moving my foot that the lady wasn't working on around in the water.

"It's not your fault, though. He raped you, Kaili. You didn't ask for this. Mark's fans will understand."

"What about Tanner? What will he think?" I looked over and Natalie had turned a knob on the side of the chair. It was vibrating and she showed me which knob to turn on mine to make it do the same. The chair started massaging my back and neck and I eased into it.

"Are you kidding? He's going to be there for you, Kaili, no matter what. Besides, Tanner adores you. You're literally all he talks about anymore," she sighed, pressing her back further into the chair.

That made me stop and think. All he talks about? *Whatever.* That's a lie. It has to be. I'm nothing special. I'm just the sad, defenseless girl who got kidnapped. I couldn't even fight the man off of me. That's nothing to be proud of.

"I am?" I asked her, embarrassingly hopeful. *Maybe she was just kidding.* She sat back in her seat with a smirk on her face. She nodded and took a drink of her coffee.

"Oh yeah. He has a massive crush on you," she smiled. I felt my cheeks getting warm and the lady started massaging one of my feet.

"I don't think so." I tucked my hair behind my ears and watched the worker.

"Does Mark know? Ya know, that Tanner likes me? If he does, I mean." I was starting to stutter, which was embarrassing.

"It's pretty obvious. Well, to everyone except your brother. But you know how oblivious he is to this sort of thing," she waved off the woman's offer of some sort of drink and looked back at me.

"Oblivious?" I asked. The woman offered me a drink, and I gladly accepted it, sitting it on the small table beside me. Natalie looked over at me puzzled and realization hit. She shook her head and frowned.

"Shoot, sorry. That means that he can't see what's right in front of him. Almost like he's blind to that kind of stuff," she explained.

I sat and thought for a few seconds. Not only was Natalie prepared to help me through an entire pregnancy, she was also telling me that Tanner has a crush on me. I didn't quite understand what 'crush' meant in the beginning, but I quickly picked up on it.

"Will you help me tell Mark about this? About me being pregnant?" I knew it was a lot to ask, but I was afraid to go at it alone.

She took a deep breath and looked at the floor.

"We'll tell him together. But not until after the MTMA's. We'll tell him right after, okay?" Her voice was soft as she spoke. So *that's* the name of the award show we're going to.

*Hmm.*

"That's a few days away," I frowned.

"Exactly. That will give us time to warm up to telling him. I know it won't be easy for you," she grabbed my hand. I nodded my head, letting the conversation end there.

The phone Mark gave me vibrated in my sweatshirt pocket and I was thankful for the distraction from the woman rubbing my feet with a rough rock. Tanner texted me asking what color dress I was going to get and I asked Natalie what to say back.

She smiled at me when I said Tanner had texted me. She suggested that he and I go to the awards together with her and Mark as sort of a double date type thing, but we aren't dating. I'm just Mark's little sister.

"Well we're going dress shopping when we get done here, so just tell him you don't know yet," she smiled. I typed back what she told me to say and sent it, putting my phone back in my pocket.

The fake nails they gave me looked really good, but they were longer than what I wanted. Natalie says I'll get used to them by the end of the day, but I'm more afraid of messing them up than anything else. They were expensive, too, and I didn't understand why.

# twenty
## Kaili

After we got our nails done, Natalie took me to a really fancy dress shop. All of the walls were lined with all sorts of dresses in all different colors. I had no idea there were so many different dress styles.

"Mmhmm. Red is *definitely* your color."

The voice came from behind me and I jumped. Natalie and I both turned at the same time and her face lit up.

"Harold!" She shouted and threw her arms around the small man. He chuckled and returned her gesture and I finally got a good look at him. His bright white hair and tan skin were a strangely wonderful contrast to his dark purple suit. He looked about 40 years old and was as short as me.

"Natalie, my dear! How are you?" He yelled, letting go of her after what felt like forever.

"I'm fantastic! But my friend Kaili here needs a dress." Her smile was massive and seemed exaggerated.

"What's the occasion?" Harold asked her while eyeing my body figure. I felt extremely uncomfortable, but that's normal for me I suppose.

"The MTMA's. Her and I are going with Tanner and Mark." Natalie's answer distracted me from Harold's judgmental glare.

"Hmm... Something fancy and formal, yet fun and energetic. Like I said, red is her color. It will compliment her skin tone. Follow me."

He walked quite fast for a man with such short legs. We followed him to a small corner in the back of the shop where the walls were lined with different types of red dresses. He thumbed through the racks and hummed along to the song playing on the radio.

"Ahh, here we go. Come try this on," he handed me a short dress and lead me to a dressing room.

Once the door was closed and I was alone, I finally looked at the material. It was rather short with no shoulder straps and in a shade of red I had never really paid attention to before. It had a silver belt going all the way around it sitting just below the breast cups. It really was a gorgeous dress, but not really my style. Not like I had much of a 'style' to begin with. I put it on anyway and looked in the mirror.

A faint knock came to the door and I looked over.

"Can I come in, sweetheart?" Harold's voice came through the wood. I opened the door for him and he gasped when he saw the dress.

"It's perfect! Do you love it?" He seemed so excited. I shrugged my shoulders and looked back in the mirror.

All my bruises and scars were showing and I felt self-conscious with my appearance. I didn't fill out the dress like I imagine Natalie would and it barely covered my scraped up knees. Harold's hands landed on my shoulders and he smiled at me through the mirror.

"It doesn't cover the marks on my skin," I folded my arms over my stomach and frowned.

"Oh hush. Those can be covered with make-up. *You* look absolutely stunning. Just look at you." He was being polite, and I would be lying if I said his words didn't make me feel a little bit better about myself.

I quietly thanked him and he helped me adjust the silver belt to fit me right. I wouldn't have let him touch me that way, but Natalie told me before we got here that it's okay because he's married to a man. I didn't understand why, but then again I didn't have to.

He straightened his suit jacket and smiled at me in the mirror.

"Are you sure this is the one you want? It's your choice, hon," he asked me. I nodded and tucked my hair behind my ear. He clasped his hands together and smiled.

"You look gorgeous, sweetie," he complimented me.

"It needs to come in around your waist more but I can fix that later. Tanner is going to just die when he sees you in this dress," he winked and I watched my cheeks turn red in the mirror. I thanked him and he walked out to let me change. Natalie came in before I could, though, and gasped just as loud as Harold did.

"Kaili you look hot!" She smiled and I giggled at her.

"Come on. Mark wants us to meet him at the hotel and order Chinese for dinner." She clapped her hands in excitement, leaving so I could finally change.

I paid Harold for my dress with Mark's credit card and he gave me a piece of paper with all of the information on it. He told us he was going to tailor it when we leave and it will be ready to pick up in a few days.

"We'll have Lia pick it up," Natalie told him. He wrote down a few things on his little notepad and thanked us for shopping with him. I thanked him for all his help and we started to leave. I put on my sweatshirt and took a deep breath, finally feeling secure in the material.

"Baby doll, it's hotter than Hell itself out there. You don't need that sweatshirt on," Harold told me. I sighed and nodded, but hugged my arms as close to me as I could. Nobody quite understands just how much comfort this sweatshirt brings me. Nobody but Tanner.

Natalie got to the door and let out a grunt.

"Paparazzi are outside. Are you okay to get through them? I'll be right beside you I promise." She looked at me thoughtfully.

"Yeah I'll be fine. Why do they follow us around so much?" I asked her, tugging at my sweatshirt sleeves. She hesitated opening the door and walked back over to me.

"They get paid to do it. Since Mark is so famous, everyone wants good pictures of him, but it gets really old after a while. They follow him everywhere," she complained.

"But he's not here, so why are they?" I pondered.

"They want pictures of you. You're his long lost little sister. People love you." She adjusted her purse on her shoulder and looked back outside at the large group of photographers. We both took a big deep breath and headed outside, ignoring the camera flashes.

"Kaili! Over here!"

"Are you dating anyone?"

"Kaili, where's your brother?"

"Look over here!"

They all seemed to be shouting the same thing at me. I held onto Natalie and tried my best to hide my face from them. A few of them looked a little bit like him, and I couldn't seem to get out of there fast enough.

The photographers pushed and shoved to get pictures of us. It was all too overwhelming and I could feel myself slipping into an all-out panic. I held tighter to Natalie's arm and she started yelling at them to move. They didn't, though. In fact, they came closer.

"Back up!" Natalie yelled again and I felt her body jerk. I decided to close my eyes and trust her completely. My hands were balled into fists as I held onto her and walked wherever she was leading me.

"Are you okay?" Her voice was softer than when she was yelling at the photographers.

"No."

# twenty-one
## Tanner

Kaili and Natalie are going to be here any minute and for some reason, I'm nervous. I can't decide if it's because of what tomorrow is or if it's because of Kaili. She makes me nervous and on-edge. It's weird. I've never felt like this before.

"Hey man," Mark came in and sat down on the couch. He put his feet on the coffee table and I cringed.

"You alright? You've been acting kinda weird the last few days," he asked. I knew exactly what he meant, but I was going to try my best to deny it. I know he'll sniff it out eventually, but hopefully not today.

"Uhh…"

The door opened before I could finish my thought and Natalie lead Kaili in the room with an arm around her shoulders. She looked terrified and on the verge of tears. Mark stood up and Kaili shook her head before running into the bathroom.

"What happened?" Mark asked before I could. Natalie sat her stuff on the floor and sunk down against the door.

"Paparazzi were everywhere. They crowded us and she had a panic attack in the car," Nat had tears in her eyes as she told us. My chest tightened. Mark started towards the bathroom, but I stopped him.

"Let me, please. Nat needs you," I pleaded with my best friend. I want to be the one who's there for her. I want to comfort her.

He hesitated, but nodded and kneeled down beside his girlfriend.

I tapped on the bathroom door and heard Kaili sobbing on the other side. I opened the door slowly, careful not to startle her. She was sitting on the floor hugging her legs and hiding her face in her knees.

I could see wet spots on the hoodie I gave her from her tears. Sitting beside her, I could feel her body shaking. She leaned into me and I sighed, taking her into my arms. She was trembling and I felt terrible.

"Hey," I tried to get her attention but her head dug into my chest even further. I pulled her closer to my body as she cried.

"They looked just like him," she whispered.

"I know. It's alright. I'm here. I won't let them get to you," I tried to calm her down. My heart broke for her. She doesn't deserve this. Nobody does.

I sat with her and let her cry for a few more minutes before she finally lifted her head to look at me.

"I hate this. I hate being scared." Her eyes were blood-shot and her cheeks were wet. I ran my thumbs against her cheeks to help dry them and she closed her eyes. She sighed and I frowned at her.

"I hate seeing you so scared. It sucks knowing that there's nothing I can do to take those memories away," I admitted to her. She wiped under her nose with a piece of toilet paper and sighed again.

"This helps," she tried to smile slightly, pulling on the hem at the bottom of the hoodie. *My hoodie helps her?* That's why I gave it to her in the first place but I didn't expect it to work as well as she's insisting.

She looks so broken. So afraid. And I hate it. I hate that I can't make it all better. I care about her so much, too much maybe. And I can't help but feel a little better knowing the hoodie helps her just like it helped me.

She sat up and wiped her face with her sleeves and took a deep breath.

"Are you okay?" I asked her, leaving one hand on her back. She let out a short breath and shook her head. My hand started rubbing circles in her back and she looked back up at me.

"Why does everyone always ask me that?" She asked and her eyes looked tired. I sat silent for a few moments. Trying to think of what to say was like trying to explain the unexplainable.

"Well, I ask because I know you're not. If someone you don't know or feel comfortable with asks if you're okay, you're supposed to just say yes even if you're not. It's just a common question for people to ask, I guess. But if someone like me, Mark, Nat, or Lia asks you, we aren't asking to see if you're okay. We ask to see if you want to tell us all the reasons you aren't."

My answer was way more loaded than I think she was expecting. Her eyes drifted to the floor and she pursed her lips together in thought.

"Why do you care so much?" She didn't sound bitter when she asked this. She sounded curious, longing for just the right answer. I had to sit and think about it for a second before turning the question towards her with, "How could I not?"

She didn't speak for a while. I imagine she was just as lost in thought as I was. Every now and then, she would look at her finger nails and pick at the sides of them before looking at me for a split second.

I was at a loss for words trying to think of things to say to her. I didn't want to tell her how I felt, mostly because I was confused as to what those feelings meant. I keep putting off talking to Mark about it, mostly because I know he'll strangle me. That's his baby sister.

Speaking of baby siblings, tomorrow is my little brother's death anniversary. I wonder what he would think of me now that I've grown up and made something of myself. I wonder if he'd like Kaili as much as I do.

"Tanner?"

Her voice woke me from my daydreaming and I looked down at her.

"Hmm?" I mumbled. She smiled a little and I couldn't help but smile with her. Her dimples showed and I resisted the urge to reach out and touch them.

"Are you okay?" She asked.

*Am I?*

# twenty-two
## Kaili

The basement seemed to be smaller than I remember. It smelled like blood and alcohol and the air was thick and hazy. The old boxes and bags were still stacked to the ceiling and the razor blade I used time and time again was laying on the floor by my feet.

I heard the front door swing open upstairs and my body stilled. My heart beat faster and faster as I silently counted the steps in my head. Eight steps. The basement door swung open and crashed into the wall, making me jump.

"I'm home, baby."

His voice was deep and slow as he came running down the stairs in the orange jumpsuit from the jail. His hands were handcuffed in front of him and he held a wicked smile. I couldn't move. I was frozen in place. He ran after me and I tried to scream, but no noise came out.

*What's wrong with me?*

His hands wrapped around my neck and he threw me to the ground, straddling me. His face twisted in anger and I tried to scream again. I shut my eyes and felt his hands roaming all over my body before he ripped my shirt down the middle.

I threw my head around and raised up, covered in sweat. The hotel bed was a jumbled mess and it was dark. My chest was tight and tears were running down my face. My body shook as I cried harder than I have in a long time. *Thank God, it was just a dream.*

"Mark?" I called out but got no reply. He must be sleeping. The clock on the wall read "3:30 am" and I sighed. *Great.* I knew there was no way I would go back to sleep, so I took a quick shower and decided to walk around the hotel lobby to keep my mind off it.

The only person in the lobby was a hotel worker cleaning around the breakfast bar.

"Ah, your friend is in the gym," the worker spoke up, looking over her shoulder at me.

"Who?" I asked her.

"That boy who came in with you and your brother. Really tall. Dark hair. Handsome young fella. He had me open the gym for him a while ago." She pointed towards the gym door and I thanked her by nodding my head and smiling.

"I'm sorry, Allen!"

*What?*

I opened the door slowly and heard a chain rattling and what sounded like an animal grunting. I looked around and eventually found a large punching bag hanging from the ceiling and a tall boy standing in front of it, breathing heavily. Even from the dim light I knew it was Tanner. The muscles in his back flexed as he hit the bag, making it swing from side to side. I stepped a little closer and could hear him crying.

"I'm so sorry Allen," he cried softly as he wrapped his arms around the punching bag. He buried his face in his shoulder and I watched his body shake with sobs.

"Who's Allen?" I asked timidly.

He whipped around and his eyes widened when he saw me. His fists balled up at his sides. They were covered in white tape and his shorts were hanging low on his hips.

"Kaili. What are you doing up? It's like four in the morning."

"I… Uhh… I had another bad dream," I answered. His breathing was intense and he had sweat dripping off the tip of his nose. His chest was rising and falling rapidly and I couldn't help but stare at him. The length of his body was intimidating, yet I felt safer with him than I did without him. I feel safe with Mark, too, but this is a different feeling and I can't decide if I like it or not.

"Why are you boxing?"

He seemed a little worried to answer me as he looked me in the eye, pulling the tape off his hands. He pointed his finger at his hip to a small tattoo I hadn't paid attention to before. A small cross on a hill was inked into the tan skin on his hipbone. In the wood of the cross were the numbers 10 and 26. Under the cross in the grass was the quote, "When I get where I'm going…"

He let out a deep sigh and I met his eyes again.

"Today's October 26th."

His face turned into a frown and his chin quivered as he spoke. I furrowed my eyebrows at him, hoping he'd catch the hint and tell me more. He took a seat on the floor and patted the floor mat beside him.

The way he looked up at me nearly broke my heart. I dropped down beside him and he sniffled.

"My little brother Allen passed away on October 26th, 2006. He was only seven years old." His voice was groggy and tired. His hands rested in his lap and his eyes stayed focused on them.

"Why don't you have the year on it?" I asked. He shook his head and a tear rolled down his face.

"I don't like keeping track of how many years it's been since he passed," he frowned and wiped his forehead with his arm. A brief moment of courage gave me the push to grab his hand in mine, which he laced his fingers into immediately.

"He was my best friend. And when he was diagnosed with cancer, I was crushed. Like, why did God want to take my little brother away from me? I didn't understand it. So I started punching my dad's old bag in the garage and Allen would watch me. It helped me keep my mind off of it and I got to spend some time with him before he went away.

"But he always watched me and talked to me. Like when I would get upset at his appointments and stuff, he'd always say 'It's okay! I'm okay! Just hit Daddy's punching bag when we get home and you'll feel better' and it just kind of stuck with me. He would try and do it with me sometimes but he was pretty weak. He couldn't do much.

"And while I boxed, he'd always say stuff like 'when I get where I'm going, I'll get to eat ice cream every day' or 'when I get where I'm going, I'll get to see Grandma again' and he always had such a bright smile and good attitude about everything. Like he had no idea he was going to die." His body started shaking and I squeezed his hand. He covered his face with his other hand and cried into it.

"It's okay," I whispered and leaned against him. I put my head on his shoulder and ran my thumb up and down his hand. He hiccupped and squeezed his eyes shut before taking a deep breath and speaking again.

"That's around when I got the sweatshirt, too. I bought it because he really liked the smiley face on it." He tried to smile down at me, but his face held a frown.

"And it didn't help the situation at all when Mom and Dad told me they were getting a divorce right before he passed away. It's like they only stayed together to see if he would make it through it. It was shitty the way they did it and I truly hated them both for a long time. Mostly because Dad worked a lot and was barely ever home in the first place, so I took care of Allen the best I could. And Mom moved out of the house before the divorce was final and I haven't heard from her since.

"But when Allen died I... I got pretty violent. I skipped school and stuff too, but I mostly fought whoever crossed me. I don't know why, but I did. I guess I was just upset. I don't know, but I can't help but feel like he'd be disappointed in me. And I feel like Mom leaving was my fault and he would hate me for it. I failed as a big brother; there's no other way to say it."

His shoulders slumped and he fumbled with his shorts while he spoke. He reached down to mess with his shoelace and his hand let go of mine to retie his shoe. I wanted to know what kind of cancer it was, but that wouldn't make the situation any easier to understand. He and I took a deep breath at the same time and I decided to speak up.

"He wouldn't be disappointed. You've done plenty of good things in your life. He would be proud of you, Tanner." His eyes met mine and they looked exhausted; physically and emotionally.

"I don't know," he frowned, standing up and adjusting his shorts. He turned back to me, offering a hand. I gladly took it and stood up with him and shook my head.

"Well I do. You're a great person. You've helped Mark get to where he is, you've been there for me when I needed you most, and you've made a good name for yourself. Allen would be so proud. Even if you were a terrible person, he'd still be proud because he's *your* little brother," I told him. I felt proud of myself for coming up with all of that. Every bit of it is true, but I'm still not very good at expressing what I'm thinking just yet.

His chin started quivering again and he looked at the floor. He whispered a "Thank you," as he wrapped his arms around me, pulling me close.

"I miss him so much," he cried into my hair as his arms squeezed my sore back. I ignored the pain and held the broken boy. I ran my hands up and down his back and felt tears starting to pool up in my eyes. All I was trying to do was soothe him, although I'm sure I wasn't helping much. I think the hug helped me more than it did him.

We stood in each other's arms for a few minutes before he raised his head and rested his forehead on mine. His eyes were closed, so I closed mine too. His breathing slowed and my heart beat increased with every second I was in his arms. His forehead came off of mine and he pressed his lips to it.

"We should probably go back to our rooms. It's four something in the morning," he grumbled. My knees threatened to buckle as he suddenly let go of me.

"Yeah, probably." I tried to mask the sadness in my voice with a yawn.

"Are you gonna be able to go back to sleep or do you want me to stay up with you?" He picked up the tape he had around his knuckles and threw the wad in a trash bin.

"I don't know. I'll probably just try and stay awake until Lia wakes us up. What about you?" I watched his stomach stretch as he lifted his shirt above his head. He let it fall over his torso and he bounced on his toes a few times.

"I can't go to sleep after I box. I've tried so many times, but my body just won't allow it. So I'll probably just take like a really long shower and watch a movie or something. You can watch a movie with me if you want."

Within a five hour span, we managed to watch two movies and I told Tanner more about what I had been through. He didn't push me to tell me like everyone else seems to be doing. He simply listened. I cried a few times while talking and he cried with me. He promised me that everything would be easier soon, and that we will get through it together.

# twenty-three
## Mark

Lia suggested relaxing the entire day yesterday, and we all happily obliged. I didn't know just how tired I was until I had the chance to just sit around for a whole day. Touring is very stressful, but I wouldn't be where I am today if it wasn't for the fans who pay to see me.

Kaili's anxiety attack two days ago really grabbed my attention. It made me realize that she's not going to heal on her own and I wish I could have been there for her. But I'm glad Tanner was there to help. They've grown pretty close the past weeks. I know my best friend well enough to say that he's battling with his feelings towards her. He hasn't talked to me about it and I don't want to confront him about it until he figures it out himself.

Today is the MTMA's and I'm more nervous than ever. Kaili still hasn't seen me perform in front of an audience, so tonight is very important. She and Natalie have been getting ready for about an hour now, and I have yet to take a shower. I guess I should probably do that since we have to leave in an hour. Lia is already dressed in her best business suit and sitting on my hotel couch, typing on her laptop.

"Why don't you ever wear dresses to these things?" I asked her. She looked up over the screen and smirked.

"I don't like dresses. I feel more professional in suits anyway," she answered.

Kaili stepped into my room looking really nervous. Her hands were folded together, her thumbs moving around.

"Mark, can I talk to you?" She asked. Lia looked up at her and picked up her stuff to leave the room. The door clicked shut and I noticed Kaili flinch at the sound.

"Yeah what's going on?" I asked.

She sat down beside me and I took in her appearance. She had makeup on and her hair was fixed but she was in a tee shirt and pair of sweats. She kept looking at the floor and I grew anxious. She held her hands in her lap and finally looked up at me with tears in her eyes.

"Kaili, talk to me." I grabbed her hands and tried to keep her eyes locked with mine.

"I was gonna wait till later to tell you this, but I just can't keep it to myself anymore." She wiped under her nose and shook her head.

"What's going on?" I urged her. She shook her head and took a deep breath. I noticed her lip quivering, so I held her hands in front of me.

"I'm... I'm pregnant," She burst into tears the moment the words left her mouth. My jaw dropped and my heart seemed to stop beating completely.

*She's what?!*

Her body started shaking and she tried to take deep breaths. I held tighter to her hands and breathed with her, hoping it would bring her out of the anxiety attack. She kept her head down and her eyes closed.

"Is it..." I didn't have to finish the question before she nodded quickly.

"I'm so sorry Mark," she cried and I held her hands to my chest.

"For what? You can't help that he raped you. It's okay. We're going to be okay. I promise." I made the promise not only to her but also to myself. We're going to be okay.

I wrapped my arms around her as she sobbed and couldn't avoid the burning in the back of my throat at the thought of the sick son of a bitch touching my sister.

"You need to tell the judge tomorrow when we go to court," I told her after a few minutes. She nodded and sniffled, wiping under her nose.

She didn't talk much after that and I left her sitting on the couch to take a shower. Just her and her baby, that is.

# twenty-four
## Mark

We rode to the arena via limo and I tried to push all personal issues to the back of my mind. Tonight is all about the performance and, if I happen to win any awards, my acceptance speeches. Clearing my mind seems to be way easier said than done.

Tanner was sitting beside me staring at his phone when he nudged me. I looked down and saw a split image of Bradley Michaels and myself followed by a short article.

"Get that crap outta here," I scolded him. He shook his head.

"Trust me, you want to read this one," he shoved the phone into my hand and glared at me. *Uh oh.* I held the phone closer to my face and started reading the article.

*Since Mark Taylor's younger sister Kaili was found on October 5th, his fandom has been nothing less than an emotional support group for the two reconnected family members. Unfortunately this hasn't set so well with another young pop star. Nineteen-year-old Bradley Michaels came to us with his exclusive opinion on the matter, claiming "Mark is using his little sister for fame".*

*"He's using the entire situation to his advantage. People love stories like that. It's all for*

*publicity. It's pathetic that he has to use his little sister to get people to like him."*

*Sounds like Bradley is a little bitter about the whole thing, but we'll see how Mark reacts to these accusations when we see him on Saturday night at the MTMA's. Follow us on all social media to be the first to know when Mark gives his comments.*

I clinched my jaw and handed Tanner back his phone. *That prick Bradley has some nerve.*

"Why'd you show me that?" I snapped at Tanner.

"I didn't want you to be blindsided by reporters tonight, alright? Just shake it off, man," he punched my shoulder.

Although he had a point, I was still pissed that he showed me. If Bradley has something to say to me, he needs to man up and say it to my face. And *I'm* supposedly the pathetic one?

*Ha.*

*Says the guy who went to a magazine to give his opinion instead of to me personally. What a wimp.*

"What happened?" Nat asked. I grabbed her hand and squeezed it.

"I'll tell you later," Tanner told her. She nodded and I kissed her knuckles.

Nat and I walked the carpet first, holding hands and smiling for the cameras. A few reporters stopped us and talked to us and I kept an eye on Tanner and my sister. She seemed pretty nervous in the limo and I hope this isn't too much for her. The last thing I want to do is make her uncomfortable. Tanner's with her, but I'm still her brother.

"Mark Taylor and Natalie Rhodes! You two look amazing!" A chipper voice made me snap my head forward. A reporter I have never seen before stood in front of us with a mound of makeup plastered to her face. That's the one thing I don't like about awards shows; all the fakeness.

"Thank you," I smiled at her and held tighter to Nat's hand.

"Let's talk about the one thing on everyone's mind lately. How's having your sister back?" She asked, shoving the silver microphone in my face.

"It's unbelievable. She went through so much and I'm so incredibly proud of her for staying strong through everything. I can't explain how happy I am to have her back in my life," I smiled genuinely. I looked over at Nat and she was already smiling at me.

"That's awesome. Everyone is happy for you both and we can't wait to learn more about her. But I have to know; what are your thoughts on Bradley Michaels' comments we all saw in the magazines this afternoon?" The woman asked, making my blood boil a little. I bit my lip and sighed.

"I think that if he has something he'd like to say to me, he shouldn't be hiding behind a magazine. Thank you."

I finished my statement and pulled Nat past the reporter and closer to the building. I looked back and saw Kaili and Tanner smiling and walking past Justin Stewart. I made a mental note to go see him later.

"Breathe, Mark," Nat pulled on my arm. I looked over at her and she looked worried. I nodded and took a few deep breaths.

"Let it go, alright? You don't want to be upset when you perform. Not tonight." Her voice was soothing and gentle. I really picked a good one. I hope my parents would be proud.

We waited for the other two to catch up before we found our seats. I held tight to Nat's hand and watched as Kaili looked around the arena. She was so amazed and it humbled me. I'm so used to playing these big arenas and here is someone who's never seen one before.

"It's big, huh?" I asked Kaili once we all sat down. She nodded eagerly and looked straight up.

"This place is huge! What's it called?" She asked. I looked up with her and thought for a second. I've performed here numerous times, but I always had trouble remembering names of arenas.

"Ceol Hall! It's a very historic music building." I turned around at the sound of Justin Stewart's voice. He was sitting right behind Kaili's seat with his manager. I smiled at my old friend and he stuck his hand out to me to shake. I shook it and he looked over at Kaili.

"Kaili, this is Justin Stewart. Justin, my sister," I introduced them and Justin shook her hand.

"It's a real pleasure to meet you, Kaili," he smiled at her.

"Justin is a famous radio host," I bragged and he smiled at me.

"I wouldn't say 'famous' but a few people know my name," he laughed and Kaili smiled politely.

"I'd love to have you back in the studio, Mark. The entire world is buzzing about your sister being back and I want to be the first to talk to you about it. That is, if you're comfortable, Kaili," Justin spoke to both of us and I tensed up a bit. Kaili looked at me and I smiled, reassuring her that it was okay.

"Do I have to say anything on the radio?" She asked him.

"You don't have to if you don't want to. I certainly don't want to make you feel uncomfortable in any way." Music slowly grew louder as it came out of the speakers and Justin patted my shoulder before looking towards the stage.

"Are you going to do the interview?" Kaili asked me quietly and I shrugged.

"He'll have to get with Lia and find out what's free on my schedule, but I wouldn't mind. He's a good guy." I told her and watched as Todd Mason took the stage.

"Who's that?" Kaili asked. Todd started throwing out jokes about everyone in the building and I couldn't help but chuckle at his crack at Bradley Michael's lack of a music career.

"That's Todd Mason. He's the most popular comedian right now," I explained to her.

"And right down here I see Mark Taylor sitting with his beautiful little sister. I don't have any jokes about you, man. I'm sure everyone in here knows you could end my career just for looking at you funny. Everyone give them a round of applause." Todd pointed down at us and Kaili looked up at him. The entire arena erupted in claps and cheers as everyone around us stood to their feet. Kaili and I stood up as well and she held my arm.

"Why are they clapping for us?" She asked me. I shrugged my shoulders and clapped with the crowd.

"They're not clapping for me; they're clapping for you." I clapped harder and she looked around the room. Countless celebrities and their management teams were clapping and smiling at her. Screams were heard from every corner of the building and I watched her look around, taking it all in.

"But what did I do? I'm just your sister," she asked, confused. I shook my head and touched her arm.

"You stayed alive. That's all you had to do," I smiled at her as a tear rolled down my cheek. She smiled back at me and we looked around the arena together and back up at Todd.

The clapping died down after a few more seconds and everyone sat down. Todd announced the first act of the show and everyone became engrossed in the performance.

# twenty-five
## Tanner

After a few of the awards were announced and several acts had already performed, Lia called Mark backstage to get ready. We all followed behind and sat in his dressing room while he changed in the bathroom. Nat went out of the room and left Kaili and I alone. Well, almost alone. Mark's body guard Dave is here too.

I flipped on the television and it was streaming the live interviews that were taking place behind the stage. Bradley was being interviewed by the same woman who had interviewed Mark earlier.

"I spoke with Mark Taylor earlier tonight and he called you out. He said to us, 'If he has something to say about me, he can come say it to my face'. What do you have to say about that?" She asked him. His face was smug as he answered.

"He talks a big game. I think it's funny how he hasn't even defended his sister in all of this. He's using her for more fame and money. It's sad he has to do that, but when you're fading out of the spotlight I guess you gotta do what you gotta do."

*Alright, buddy.* You've messed with the wrong people. The only one who can talk crap about my best friend is me. That's it. Nobody else. Anyone who thinks they can run their mouths like that deserve to be

140

taught otherwise. I stood up and Kaili looked away, fumbling with her fingers.

"Where do you think you're going?" Dave asked as I went towards the door.

"Going to teach that little twerp a lesson," I declared. He grabbed my arm and held me back.

"Like hell you are," he gripped my arm tighter.

"He's talking shit about Kaili! He has no right to say that crap. He doesn't even know her," I pointed to Kaili and she sat with her legs folded beside her body in a way that made her look smaller. Her expression was unreadable as she fumbled with my sweatshirt in her lap.

"I understand that, but you can't just walk up to him and knock him out." Dave tried to get me to look at him, but I focused on the door behind him. I could slowly feel my body going stiff in anger and I knew if I didn't get to Bradley quick, I'd take it out on Dave.

"Like hell I can't."

I shook loose of Dave's grip and walked out of the dressing room. *Deep breaths, Tanner. You can't kill the kid.* I'll admit my actions are rather hasty, but I don't care at this point. All I care about was ending this nonsense as quickly as possible.

I walked further down the hall and entered the main lobby area, searching for him. I mentally prepared myself for when I find him. I just kept thinking about what he was saying about Kaili. She doesn't deserve that. She's incredible.

The lobby was packed with all sorts of people. I dodged and passed many A-list celebrities and saw an interviewer out of the corner of my eye. It was a different woman than before. Bradley was standing in front of her as she smiled at the cameras. *Bingo*.

"Bradley, tell me, what is this feud you're having with Mark Taylor?" The woman beamed, her synthetic smile on full display. If I wasn't so mad at Bradley, I'd tell her to cut the crap and treat him like a normal person. There's no need to be fake around all of these people.

"It's not really a feud. I just think he's using his sister for attention," Bradley shrugged. *His freaking nerve*. He keeps repeating himself like the ignorant moron he is.

I couldn't concentrate, I was so furious. My blood was boiling as he switched his weight from one foot to the other. Even his body movements were making me mad. I need to release this anger now or I'm going to explode.

"How?" The woman asked, looking genuinely confused. She must be getting paid pretty good to pretend to not know about and actually care about all of this crap. He shrugged his shoulders.

"He's using the story for attention. She's all over the magazines and stuff. It's sad, really. Not only is he using it for attention, but she's probably using him for money while she whores around with older men like the guy who kidnapped her," he spoke nonchalantly, a look of disgust on his face.

That did it.

I strode right up to him, slammed my hands onto his chest, and clutched his collar in my fists. My knuckles were turning white and my heart was beating out of my chest. The smug look on his face disappeared when his eyes locked with mine.

"Listen here, you lying sack of shit. That girl has gone through way more than your pathetic little mind can even begin to imagine. She was in a basement for eight years. *Eight fucking years*. And I refuse to let you walk all over her. *You* are a piece of shit and if I see you get anywhere near her, I swear on my life it will be the last thing you do," I spat through my teeth.

To say he was shocked would be a massive understatement. He nodded his head quickly and I dropped him on the ground. I hadn't realized I had picked him up, but clearly I do stupid things when I'm mad.

"Sorry," I mumbled towards the interviewer and she flicked her head to the side, signaling that I needed to leave. I nodded and walked away. I heard a few gasps and someone say "that was crazy," and I couldn't fight the overwhelming feeling of accomplishment. Bradley got what was coming for him.

I stepped back into the dressing room and Kaili was sitting on the couch in the same position I left her in. She kept her eyes on her lap and I noticed she didn't have my sweatshirt with her anymore.

"Are you alright?" I asked quietly. She kept her face down, but I knew she heard me. She just wouldn't look at me.

"Damn it, Tanner. I told you not to hit him," Dave boomed as he slammed the door behind me. I turned to him and he folded his arms over his chest.

"I didn't hit him, though. I just kinda picked him up," I defended, mimicking how I held his collar with my hands. He raised an eyebrow and shook his head.

"I told you not to touch him, and now look what you've done," he griped, turning to the live streaming TV in the corner of the room. A replay of me getting in Bradley's face was playing and Mark stormed into the room.

"What the hell was that?" He growled at me. Kaili was silent and I was praying that she wasn't mad at me. I sighed and smashed my lips together. He gave me a look that I knew meant I better start explaining before he hit me.

"He was saying a bunch of bull about you and Kaili. He was saying she's fake and I took care of the problem," I answered. He sighed and ran his hand through his hair.

"That little son-of-a-," he started.

"Mark, it's okay," Kaili interrupted and I was surprised she spoke. Mark bunched his fists up and I took a step back. I've never seen him this mad before.

"No it's not! I should go out there and kick his ass," he raised his voice slightly, but never loud enough to be considered yelling.

"You don't need to get in trouble," she tried to persuade him quietly. He shook his head and ran his tongue over his lips. I sat down on the couch next to Kaili, stretching my fingers. They were a little sore from holding Bradley up by his stupid blue shirt.

"I don't care if I get in trouble or not! You're my sister. I'm supposed to take care of you. And if that

144

means beating the shit out of that little punk on national television, then so be it."

He was furious, and I sure as hell wasn't about to get in his way. He paced around for a few seconds before focusing on Kaili, like I should have in the first place. He finally sat down on a chair and took a few deep breaths to calm down. I watched his shoulders slump and the door swung open.

"Dang, Tanner! You scared the crap out of him!" Nat gushed as she walked in. She looked at Kaili, who was sitting as far away from me as she could get without getting off the couch.

"Are you okay, honey?" She asked Kaili, who looked up at her and shook her head.

"I don't want to go back out there," she spoke. *Shit*. She's not mad; she's afraid.

That's just *fantastic*.

Lia walked in the room with a security guard trailing behind her.

"Tanner…" She started but I put my hands up in defense.

"Don't. I know," I sighed, defeated. She came over to me and slapped the back of my head.

"That's for acting like a child. But I have to admit, I'm glad you did it before I got the chance to," she scolded, then praised. I knew I liked Lia for a reason. She sat down between Kaili and I and smiled at me.

"Mark, you're on in five minutes," a stage manager spoke, poking his head in the room. Mark hopped to his feet and looked over at me.

"We're not done talking about all this shit, alright? You better not leave this room without me knowing," he looked at me threateningly and I froze. *Whoa. What'd I do to him?*

He walked out of the room with Nat and Lia following him. I looked over at Kaili and she had her head on a pillow and tears in her eyes.

"Kaili, please talk to me. What's wrong?" I asked her, touching her leg. She flinched away from me and my heart lurched. *I caused that*. And that feels so much worse than Bradley Michaels could say about her.

# twenty-six
## Mark

*Freaking Tanner.*

Not only did he get to Bradley before I could, but he also scared Kaili in the process. I saw the look on her face when I came in the room. She was *terrified*. I don't know if what he did reminded her of some day in the basement or what happened, but I know it was Tanner's fault. He should have never left that dressing room.

I stood under the stage on the platform and took a deep breath.

"Mark!" I turned at the sound of Kaili's voice. She stood about six feet away with Dave standing beside her. She held her arms over her stomach and I could sense her anxiety.

"What are you doing here? I thought you wanted to stay in the dressing room," I yelled over the announcers' voices coming out of the speakers. She shrugged and looked up at Dave.

"She wanted to watch you sing," he told me, placing his hand on her back. She leaned closer to him and nodded her head.

That made me smile. She smiled back and I took a deep breath and looked around the room to see if I could see any place for her to watch me safely when I got an idea.

"Dave, take her up to the balcony suite. Don't let anyone near her, alright? I want to be able to see her at all times," I told him. He nodded and escorted her away. Within two minutes, I could see her smiling and waving at me from the balcony. I waved back and waited impatiently to be announced.

"And we're live in five... four... three... two..." The stage manager counted down beside me and the music started.

The platform raised slowly and I stood up, causing the crowd the scream and cheer. As I sang, I saw Kaili holding her hands over her mouth and tears streaming down her face.

I couldn't stop smiling as I sang the words and saw Natalie show up beside Kaili on the balcony. They danced together and waved down at me. I closed my eyes for a huge high note and heard the crowd cheering. I felt proud of myself as I noticed everyone singing along to my lyrics. It's truly an incredible feeling.

Once I finished the song, the crowd erupted and Todd Mason came back to the stage to stand beside me. He gave me a hug and kept one hand on my shoulder as we looked over the screaming crowd together.

"Wow! Give it up for Mark Taylor!" He yelled into his microphone and the floor shook from all the screaming. I smiled widely and waved at a few of my famous friends.

"It's an honor to be here to present this award to you as well so stick around for a second. Mark Taylor, you are the first ever recipient of the

Honorable Artist Award for all the incredible work you do not only in music but in all your charity work over the years. All of your hard work is greatly appreciated, Mark. Congratulations, man," Todd spoke into his mic, handing me a shiny award. He clapped along with the crowd as I smiled at the award. My breathing was shallow from performing and I took a second to try to catch up with myself.

"Wow. Never in a million years did I think I would be in this spot right now. I thank God every day for this amazing opportunity to do what I love and I can't thank Him enough for all of this. To my manager and record label, thank you for believing in me. Thank you to my fans for never leaving my side. Thank you Tanner and Natalie for being the best friends I could ever ask for and being the family I haven't had in years."

"And Kaili..." I looked up at her in the balcony and she was crying. Natalie put her arm around her and laid her head on Kaili's. I wiped under my eyes and took a deep breath.

"I'd like to apologize to you for a few things. I'm sorry I couldn't stop that man from taking you from us. I'm sorry I couldn't protect you like a big brother should. I'm sorry I couldn't find you. I'm sorry I've lived this insane life while you were stuck in a basement fighting for your life. And I'm sorry for bringing you into this crazy, mixed up lifestyle we're living in. I'm so proud of you. I'm proud of you for being brave these past few weeks and for those eight years I couldn't be with you. So thank you, Kaili, for never giving up. You're the strongest person I know and I can't thank that mailman enough for finding you. I love you, Sis."

And with that, I walked off the stage with tears in my eyes. The floor shook violently as the crowd roared.

I was escorted back to my dressing room where Tanner was waiting for me. He stood and I did the most honorable thing I could think to do. Despite being angry with him, I grabbed him and hugged him.

Kaili and Nat walked in shortly after and wrapped their arms around me. We all cried together and I knew I had something real with everyone in this little group. They're my own little family.

# twenty-seven
## Kaili

*"Fear; an unpleasant emotion caused by the belief that someone or something is dangerous."*

Fear seemed to be the only emotion I had for this. The courtroom was large. "Intimidating" is what my lawyer, Lewis, called it. He and Mark had met up a few hours ago to discuss my situation. He didn't want to talk to me personally until we went into the courtroom, which I thought was strange.

I sat beside him behind a small table while Mark, Tanner, and Lia sat in the audience. I looked around at all the unfamiliar faces until I saw Andrew. He was in his mailman uniform and he waved at me. I sent him a quick smile and looked back at my brother, who was showing Tanner something on his phone.

The audience seating was slowly filling up and I saw Sam in the crowd with a bright purple work outfit on and a man sitting beside her, whom I'm assuming is her husband. She waved at me and I smiled back, waving sheepishly. Then I felt a hand on my shoulder.

"Kaili, I can assure you that today is going to go perfectly. You don't have a jury, so this will be all up to the judge. Quick and easy. You have absolutely nothing to worry about," Lewis insisted. I looked over at him and he nodded.

"Thank you," I mumbled. He then handed me a plastic bag and smiled at me.

"Your friend said to give you this. He said it might come in handy for you," he chimed, sitting the bag in my lap. I untied the handles and looked inside. I could feel my heart beating faster as I recognized the gray material. My sweatshirt was inside with a small piece of paper taped to it. I opened up the small paper and read the sloppy handwriting.

*Hey Kaili. I just wanted to apologize for yesterday. I didn't mean to scare you. That was the last thing on my mind. I just wanted Bradley to learn a lesson. I swear I would never hurt you. Ever. Don't think of me as a scary person, think of me as kind of like a body guard but with cooler hair. Because that's all I was trying to do. Protect you, I mean.*

*That being said, I thought you might want this in court to make you feel better. But don't you worry about a thing. Lewis has everything under control. He might even kick the guy's butt just for the hell of it. But, it's going to be okay. How about after this, we all go back to the hotel and order pizza to celebrate? Sound like fun?*

*Mark and I are right behind you if you need us. Lia is too, but I don't think she's willing to beat up a crazy dude for you like your brother and I am. She's not that brave. She might act like she's all big and bad, but she's just a big ole' chicken. But don't tell her I told you that. She'll kick my ass.*

*Talk to you soon.*
*Tanner*

A small smiley face that looked like the one on his sweatshirt was drawn at the bottom by his name. I smiled at the note and put it in my pocket. The sweatshirt stayed folded up on my lap as I turned to look at Tanner. He was smiling at me already and Mark made a funny face.

Tanner had scared me yesterday. Nowhere close to how bad my kidnapper has scared me, but I was still afraid of him after last night. I even tried to casually give him his sweatshirt back but I'm glad he returned it to me. I missed it more than I'd care to admit to him, or anyone else for that matter.

"All rise for the honorable Judge Yates," a loud voice got everyone's attention. Everyone stood up and I looked over at Lewis. He nodded his head towards the front and a woman in a black robe stepped behind the large desk. She sat down and two of the police officers I had met at the jail house came in. They had a woman whom I'd never seen before walking behind them.

After everyone was seated, Judge Yates started talking about laws and different court related things I didn't understand. I zoned out as she spoke and kept my focus on breathing normally.

The door to the right of me opened up and several officers walked in. Officer Kelly led a man bound in chains and dressed in orange into the room. I caught a glimpse of the reason for my horrible nightmares and instantly tensed up. The man turned to look at me and my breathing seemed to catch in my throat. He walked ahead of Officer Kelly and she had him sit down at the other table with another man in a dress suit before cuffing his hands back together in front of him.

"Your honor, Anthony Ross," she turned and looked up at Judge Yates, who had her glasses dangling from her lips.

*Anthony Ross.*

My fingernails dug into the palms of my hands as I stared at him. He winked at me and turned his attention to the front of the room, but I couldn't look away. Lewis's hand went under the table and he grabbed ahold of one of my hands. He brought it to the top of the table and squeezed it gently.

"Breathe," he whispered in my ear. I turned around to look at Tanner, but his eyes were elsewhere. Mark looked at me for a second before looking straight down. I then looked to Lia for some sort of comfort and was met with her kind eyes and a warm smile.

"Everyone stand and raise your right hand…"

A police officer recited some kind of oath to us and I mumbled along, keeping my eyes on the floor.

"Okay so the defendant Anthony Ross has been in the Los Angeles County jail for the past three weeks on account of kidnapping the plaintiff, Kaili Taylor. Mister Ross kidnapped Miss Taylor in Nevada when she was 10 years old and held her hostage in his home right outside of Los Angeles for the past eight years. He has refused to feed her properly, he beat her, raped her, and verbally assaulted her countless times; mostly while intoxicated. Is all of this true, Miss Taylor?"

Judge Yates held her glasses in her hand and looked down at me. Lewis sat quietly and I nodded my head.

"Yes, ma'am," Lewis whispered. I glanced over at him and he nodded his head with wide eyes.

"Yes, ma'am," I squeaked. She nodded her head and tapped on the desk with her finger. She took a deep breath and I looked back at Mark.

"Miss Taylor, may I speak with you privately for a moment?" Her eyes peaked over the papers at me. Lewis whipped his head around and looked at me.

"Do I go?" I asked him. He nodded quickly and I stood up to follow the judge into a separate room. Officer Kelly closed the door behind us and folded her arms over her chest.

"Miss Taylor, we received documentation from a blood test that we'd like you to take a look at," Judge Yates frowned, handing me a piece of paper. I looked down at the writing and shook my head. All the words on the paper were foreign to me. *What eighteen year old girl knows all these medical terms?* Certainly not one who's been in a basement for eight years.

"I don't know what any of this means." I kept my head down and spoke quietly.

"Kaili, honey, we got ahold of your blood test results and, as the police, we had to alert the judge about this. Are you aware that you're pregnant, dear?" Officer Kelly spoke up and I looked at her.

"Yes ma'am," I admitted respectfully. Officer Kelly sighed and looked at Judge Yates. They had some sort of unspoken conversation with their eyes and I felt confused and left out.

"Since you're now a little over four months pregnant, you had to have been underage when you conceived. With that being said, you will be funded by

155

the state for child support while Anthony Ross is in prison. We have to add this to his record also as it is a major crime. Are you okay with us announcing that in the court room today?" Judge Yates' voice was noticeably less scary as she spoke this time.

"Yes ma'am. I'm sorry for not telling you." I looked back down at the floor and bit my lip. Officer Kelly touched my arm and I glanced up at her to be met with her smile.

"It's okay, Kaili. We know this isn't easy for you," she sympathized. I only nodded, noticing my hands starting to sweat.

She led us back into the court room and Tanner's eyes were on me. His eyebrows were creased together and he looked genuinely concerned.

"I'm okay," I mouthed to him. He nodded and I sat back in my chair beside Lewis. He looked over at me expectantly and Judge Yates took her seat behind the large desk again.

"The judge knows I'm pregnant," I whispered to Lewis. His eyes widened and he let out a small cough. He hit his chest with his fist and sniffled before leaning closer to me.

"Oh my. Does Mark know?" He asked. I simply nodded back and Judge Yates got our attention. She took off her glasses again and pointed them at Anthony.

"Are you aware that impregnating a minor is a major crime, Mister Ross?" She asked him. He smirked and nodded his head.

"Yes ma'am," he smiled at her. I grabbed the sweatshirt from under my seat and moved the fabric around in my hands.

"And are you aware that Miss Taylor is four months pregnant with your child?" She asked him and I heard Tanner and Lia gasp behind me. Anthony glanced back at them and smiled even wider at Judge Yates.

"I am now," he smirked. His voice was smooth when he boasted. I heard Lia cough from behind me and I turned to see Mark talking to her and Tanner quietly, more than likely explaining to them what I had told him.

"And you aren't sorry about any of this or denying any of it? Why even bring this to court? You're wasting everyone's time, sir," Judge Yates shouted at him. Anthony sat up straight in the most intimidating way. He put his cuffed wrists on the table and chuckled.

"The news wants a story so I'm letting them have one," he pointed at the cameraman standing beside a security guard, recording everything for the news.

"Besides, I wanted to see my baby one last time," he finished, smiling at me.

I felt sick. He's called me "baby" countless times while raping me and that word will forever disgust me. Judge Yates stuck her glasses back on her face and straightened up the papers in front of her before looking at Anthony's lawyer.

"Would you like to say anything?" She questioned. He shook his head at her and she looked at

Lewis. She quirked an eyebrow at him expectantly and he nodded.

"Yes, your honor." Lewis stood up and adjusted his suit before walking around the table.

"I'd like to call Anthony Ross to the stand for questioning." His voice was strong and scary, yet I felt safe knowing he was on my side.

Anthony sat in the small box space beside Judge Yates' desk and looked over at me. I took the sweatshirt in my hands and held it tight. The fabric was soft on my fingertips and I silently prayed that it would magically transport me out of this place.

"Mister Ross, is it true that you kidnapped and held this young lady hostage for eight years?" Lewis asked the first question, and I prayed as hard as I could that I'd be able to make it through without bawling my eyes out or screaming in terror.

"Yes." His voice startled me and I looked back at Mark for the umpteenth time. His eyes locked with mine and he seemed just as afraid as I was. He mouthed the words "are you okay" and I shook my head "no" before looking back at Lewis.

"Before you continue, is there really even a point in your questioning?" Judge Yates asked Lewis.

"Miss Taylor deserves to hear why he did this to her, your honor," he spoke very respectfully towards her.

"Proceed," she smiled at him. He nodded his head and turned back to Anthony.

"Why her? Why not her brother or one of her parents?" He used his hands while he spoke; moving them around in sync with his words.

"I wanted her," Anthony explained proudly. I felt like there was more to his answer than he was leading on, and that scared me. My heart started pounding harder and harder.

"Have you ever physically assaulted her or raped her?" He questioned, although Judge Yates had already said he did. I knew there was a reason for his questioning, but I wasn't quite sure how I would benefit from it.

"Yeah."

"Why?"

"She was asking for it."

I felt my body beginning to shake. His eyes were on me and I felt just like I did every time he would rape me; helpless and scared.

"How exactly was she asking for that type of abuse?"

"Why are you asking me this stuff? Everyone already knows I'm going to prison." His hands pulled at the cuffs on his wrists and he let out a frustrated grunt. He gave up and slammed his fists on the table. I jumped at his sudden outburst and kept my head down, hoping it would all be over soon.

"Just answer the damn question." I gasped at Lewis' harsh words. I heard Lia cough behind me and I slowly turned to look at her. She stuck her tongue out and crossed her eyes, which made me smile a little. She smiled back and I looked over at Tanner who was looking down at his lap, ignoring my stare.

"She wouldn't do what I told her to do." Anthony leaned back in his chair and tried to cross his arms.

"So that's asking to be raped and beaten?" I looked up at Lewis and he had his head cocked to the side, watching Anthony.

"Absolutely," he answered casually.

"So why didn't you kill her afterwards? Surely you'd thought about it." I closed my eyes as Lewis asked this.

"I had thought about it. But I knew if I killed her, I'd have nothing left of her. I couldn't give her up that easily. I had too much fun with her." My eyes stayed screwed shut. I held the sweatshirt in my hands and moved the material around my fingers. *Just breathe, Kaili. Just breathe.*

Lewis didn't say anything after that. My hands were sweating and I felt like throwing up.

"I'd like to call Kaili Taylor to the stand," Lewis declared, causing my head to raise and my heart to beat faster. Anthony stepped out of the small box space and smiled at me as he sat down behind his table.

"Kaili, honey, that means you have to come up here," Lewis whispered. He walked over to me and helped me to the small box space. I sat down and held the sweatshirt in my lap, refusing to look up.

"In your statement, you said that Mister Ross had picked you up from a Nevada truck stop, yes?" Lewis' voice went back to how it was when he talked to Anthony, and I didn't like it. But I nodded.

"Please speak, sweetie. We need verbal answers for the report," Judge Yates told me quietly. I looked up at her and she gave me a half smile. I nodded back to her and turned back to Lewis.

160

"Uhh, yes," I spoke quietly.

"And in the medical report presented to me this morning, your blood tests determined that you're four month's pregnant with Ross's child. Resulting from a rape, I'm sure. Am I correct?" The sweatshirt in my hands gave me an excuse to look down for a bit while I took a few calming breaths and counted to ten in my head.

"Yes," I heard the judge sniffle when I answered.

"Please tell us what you remember from the day he first kidnapped you."

Looking back up, I saw Lia holding onto Mark's arm. His face was red and he looked angry. Tanner looked the same, but more hurt. I know I should have told him sooner, but I didn't think they would bring it up in court. Lewis appeared in front of me and placed his hands on the edge of the small box space.

"Hey. It's okay. He can't hurt you anymore," he stated before stepping away and nodding his head at me.

"I remember being at the gas station with my family. It was late at night and there wasn't much light in the parking lot. He came out of nowhere and picked me up and threw me in the bed of his truck. I passed out and woke up the next day I guess and he was driving down a highway. He pointed a gun at my head and made me lay down. When we got to his house, he pulled me out of the truck by my hair and tried to cut my throat but I fought back. Then he threw me in the basement and locked me in there."

My breathing was shaky and my voice was squeakier than I had intended. I kept my eyes on Lewis, afraid to look anywhere else.

"Thank you, Kaili," Judge Yates dismissed me quietly. I stood up and Lewis helped me back to my seat at the table. When I sat down, I felt eyes on the back of my head. I didn't want to turn around and face Mark just yet. He knows about everything, but I'm still afraid to turn and look at him. I think more than anything I am afraid that if I turn around, I'll start screaming and demand that he take me to the hotel or anywhere but here.

Judge Yates looked down at me and I gripped the sweatshirt tighter. She frowned and looked over at Anthony.

"As a judge, I'm supposed to treat every case as fair and open-minded as I can. Just looking at this poor girl, there is no question in my mind whether what she's saying is true or false. Mister Ross isn't denying anything. I hope the best for you and your family, Kaili. In conclusion, in the case of Ross versus Taylor, Anthony Ross will serve 65 years to life in the California State Penitentiary for aggravated kidnapping, attempted murder, second degree rape of a minor, aggravated assault of a minor, impregnating a minor, and several unsolved cases of assault of an officer."

She spoke quickly and authoritatively before slamming a wooden thing on the desk, making me jump. The two officers smiled weakly at me and grabbed Anthony, leading him out of the court room.

# twenty-eight
## Kaili

"Kaili," Mark's voice came from behind me and I turned to see him jogging to me. He wrapped me in a hug and I felt a massive weight lift off my shoulders.

"You don't ever have to see him again. I promise," he croaked as he held me tight. He let go of me and smiled the biggest smile I've ever seen. Lewis shook hands with Mark and gave me a quick hug and congratulations before leaving the court room. Tanner and Lia both hugged me briefly.

Sam walked up to me slowly and I practically jumped in her arms. She held me tight and we cried together for a minute. She said she had to leave to run errands before it got too late, so her and her husband left soon after. As I grabbed ahold of Mark and Lia's hands, we started to leave when two police officer stopped us.

"Miss Taylor, this woman would like to speak with you," one officer requested, motioning to the woman I saw come in earlier.

"Kaili Taylor, meet Deborah Ross; Anthony Ross's mother," the other officer introduced us.

I looked at the woman and her face looked tired and sad. She held her hands together and frowned at me. Anthony inherited his nose and cheek bones from her, I could tell. She was quite small, which only made me wonder how big of a man his father must be.

"I'm so sorry my son did those things to you, sweetie. I had no idea he was holding you hostage." She broke out into sobs and I felt the need to hug her. I didn't, though. I let go of Lia's hand and latched onto Mark's arm, hiding slightly behind him.

"It's okay. I won't let her touch you," he whispered, leading me to come out from behind him.

Deborah sat down in the chair behind her and I sat across from her, unsure of what to do. Her cheeks were red and wet from tears. Mark scooted a chair closer to me and sat down, crossing his arms over his chest.

"Anthony was always a happy child growing up. He didn't have many friends, but he seemed content with himself. He wasn't into sports or anything like that but he loved music much like Mark," she started to speak before Mark cut her off.

"He's nothing like me. Don't compare us." His voice was sharp and Deborah flinched in her seat.

"Mark," I sighed. He grabbed my hand and held it tight. I closed my eyes and felt two large hands land on my shoulders.

"I didn't mean to offend you, Mark. I'm sorry," her voice cracked.

"Anyway, when Anthony got older, he spent a lot of time in his bedroom reading and listening to strange music. He never went out on dates. Never hung out with friends. He just stayed home all the time. I didn't mind, though. He was a good kid. He always helped me around the house and ran errands for me when I needed him too. But after he turned eighteen, he became very violent. He got in a lot of bar fights and spent many nights in jail. I don't know how he got into those bars, but he did.

"He even tried to fight me once, but the police got to him before he could. We had gotten into an argument about him moving out and he didn't take it well. He had never hit me before but I was afraid that he would this time. So I called the police and they wanted to place a restraining order on him but I wouldn't let them. What kind of mother would I be if I had a restraining order on my own son? I just couldn't do it."

Her eyes were watering and one of the police officers touched her shoulder.

"I'm okay. I'm okay," she waved her hands around to get the officer off of her. She took a deep breath and shook her head a few times.

"Ma'am, we have to leave soon," the other officer told her, grabbing her other shoulder. She threw her arm back and shot a glare towards the officer.

"I'm almost done!" She barked, which made me lean into Mark. He held my hand tighter and used his other hand to caress my arm.

"Then he disappeared. He just up and left and never came back. He had called me once since then and he told me, 'she doesn't love me, Mom, she left me for him,' and I didn't know what he meant. He didn't explain, he just hung up.

"So when I got a call from the jail, I was shocked. And all he said was, 'Mommy, I messed up. I got caught. It's over' and my heart broke for him. He told me that he kidnapped someone and the police found out. He didn't tell me he had you for eight years. Kaili I'm so sorry. I just can't… I can't believe that he'd do that to someone. He ripped you apart."

She was crying as she told the end of her story and I fought the urge to hug her again. She didn't do anything wrong, but for some reason I held her responsible for everything. She is his mother after all.

An officer handed her a tissue and she dabbed her eyes with it. She looked around the empty court room for a second and I kept my eyes locked on her. *She doesn't scare me. She didn't do anything.* I just kept telling myself that.

"Now I know this is a long shot into the darkness, but is there any way I could meet my grandbaby when you have it?" Her question was directed at me and Mark's arm tightened around me.

"I don't know if that's such a good idea," Lia remarked from behind me. Her hand touched the top of my head and Tanner let go of my shoulder. I looked back at them and shook my head.

"I don't mind," I spoke up. Mark looked at me with wide eyes. I looked up at Deborah and her eyes were filled with tears.

"It will have to be under police supervision for Kaili's safety," the officer chimed in.

"Absolutely. I understand. Thank you so much." Deborah was on her feet and hugging me in no time. My body tensed at the sudden contact but I still reached my arms around her. I didn't see any reason as to why she shouldn't see her grandbaby. She lost her son, so I was giving her a second chance. I wish I had a second chance with my life, but I didn't.

"Thank you," she whispered in my ear. I nodded my head and she let go of me to wipe her face. Officer Kelly walked up to us and clapped her hands together.

"I'm sorry to break this little meeting up, but the judge has asked us to clear the courtroom for another hearing," she announced, voice stern.

"Sure, sure. Sorry we took so long," Deborah spoke frantically, like I'd change my mind if she didn't.

"It's okay. Just head back out through the side door and down the hallway." Officer Kelly pointed in different directions as she spoke, but my eyes were fixed on Deborah.

# twenty-nine
## Anthony Ross

A life sentence isn't too bad I suppose. I have nothing else to live for. The love of my life left me for another man. They got married and had kids and now she's dead. I took their kid, got caught, thrown in jail, and there's nothing I can do about it. There's no turning back now. I'm screwed.

"That orange suit looks nice on you, Ross," the officer guiding me broke my thoughts as he locked me in a large holding cell. He slammed the door behind me and I cringed at the loud noise.

"Thanks, cupcake," I smiled back to him. He put his hands through the bars and unlocked my cuffs and chains. Once they were free, I rubbed the irritated skin and cursed him out in my mind.

"You're a sick man, you know that?" He asked me, tossing the chains onto his desk.

"I pride myself on being a sick man. So thank you." I could tell I was starting to annoy him, but I didn't care. I'm going to rot in prison anyway. Might as well have a little fun while I still can.

"You're going to big boy jail tomorrow," he taunted, walking around in front of the cell door. He took a sip of his coffee and raised the glass to me.

"Maybe I'll make some new friends. Might even get myself a sexy lady," I taunted right back and he looked at me with pure disgust. He sat at his desk and started sorting through papers. I stuck my hands through the bars and interlocked my hands together.

"Are you married?" I asked him, deciding to bug him a bit. *Why not, right?*

"I am," he quirked an eyebrow at me. I cocked my head to the side slowly like I've seen murderers do in those creepy movies I could only watch if all the lights in the house were turned on.

"Do you love her?" I prodded. He puffed up his cheeks and blew the air out.

"Yes," he answered with a smile.

"And what would you do if someone were to steal her away from you?" He thought about my question for a few seconds before sitting up straight and glaring at me.

"I'd try and get her back. Is there any reason as to why you're asking me these questions, Mister Ross?" He asked. He was officially irritated and I loved every part of it.

"Yes there is. I ask because the last time someone stole the love of my life from me, I stalked them and kidnapped their daughter," I revealed with no remorse or regret in my voice, mostly because I had neither. His eyes went wide and I gripped the bars on the door.

Emily was working her first year as a school teacher and we met at work. Sure, I was only a janitor, but she saw the potential in me. She told me I could do anything I set my mind to. She inspired me to be better. She was my life. I knew she was the one I was supposed to spend the rest of my life with. But apparently she didn't feel the same.

We had dated for a year when she met the new guy, Jason. She left me two weeks after meeting him and started dating him a month later. I was crushed.

I watched their every move. They ended up getting married and he joined the Navy, so I joined too. I never made it through boot camp, though, so I had to find another way to get to her.

I wanted to win her back so bad but she ignored me. I watched her for over 20 years just waiting for her to come back to me, but she never did. She didn't know I was watching her. She didn't know *anything*. She stayed wrapped up in her stupid husband. So I got my revenge by taking their precious Kaili.

Through the years of having Kaili in my basement, I watched Mark too. He's a worldwide superstar, so it was easy to track him. I watched all his interviews, television appearances, everything. I went to all of his concerts in a 100 mile radius and listened to him whine about not having his family.

I knew he was looking for his sister. I knew just by the way he acted on stage. And there I was, practically dangling her in front of his face. He had no idea. Nobody did. And seeing him squirm was like a drug. He would cry about his family all the time and I loved every second of it.

He said in one of his first interviews that both his parents were dead and I felt responsible. I was proud of myself for causing such a family disaster. I didn't kill them directly. Jason died in a jet accident and Emily killed herself. While it hurt knowing my love had done such a thing, I was happy I got the last laugh.

The officer didn't say much to me after I told him what I had done. In fact, he didn't say anything to me. He walked out of the room and yelled for another officer.

"Where the hell is Officer Kelly?!" He barked down the hall way. *Ooo. Officer Kelly. I'm so scared.* Note my sarcasm, if you will.

A woman in uniform walked in a few seconds later and she placed her hands on her hips. Typical woman.

"What is it, Hood?" She asked him. She looked over at me and I stuck my tongue out at her.

"Tell her what you told me." His demand was pointed at me and I placed my hand over my heart dramatically.

"I don't know what you're talking about. I've been quiet the whole time," I smirked, tracing the bars with my fingers.

"Don't even try it, Ross. Tell her now." His voice was deeper, much like a father scolding his son for backing into the mailbox with his brand new Ferrari. I want a Ferrari.

"Tell her what?" I played stupid. He started walking around the room with his hands on his hips and Officer Kelly raised her eyebrows at me. She stepped up to the bars and placed her hands on the metal above my head.

"Cut the shit, Ross. We have cameras in here and audio recorders set up everywhere, so either you tell me what you told him or I look it up on the security footage," Officer Kelly exclaimed, pointing all around at the different cameras perched in corners of the ceiling.

"Why? We were just talking. It's not like it's going to change anything," I bit back. She lowered her glare to a scowl and I winked at her.

"Because that poor girl deserves to know why you did what you did to her," Officer Hood squinted his eyes at me.

I cocked my head to the side at him and pursed my lips.

"I knew exactly who I was kidnapping when I took Kaili. Her mom, Emily, was the love of my life, but she left me for *Jason Taylor*. So, I watched them for years and thought out my revenge. What better way to get back at them than by kidnapping their kid?" Officer Kelly dropped her jaw when I told her.

She looked over at Officer Hood and he placed his hands on his hips. They are quite the pair. *LA's finest.*

"Why wasn't this mentioned in court?" Officer Kelly asked me and I shrugged my shoulders at her.

"Just didn't come up." My fingers traced over the metal door hinges and I winced when a jagged piece cut me.

"Is there anything else you'd like to tell us?" Officer Kelly crossed her arms over her chest and placed her weight on one hip. She waited impatiently for me to speak, tapping her foot in the most annoying way possible.

"I took a bunch of her stuff she threw away when she moved in with Jason and kept it in the basement where I had Kaili. There was a mirror and a bunch of old clothes Emily wore in high school. So Kaili was surrounded by her mom's stuff the whole time and had no idea."

I told them a little more information than I wanted to and watched their reactions. I knew they'd add more to my record, but what did I have to lose anyway? Might as well tell them everything. It's not like I'm getting out of here.

"Get Lia Martin on the phone," Officer Kelly ordered Officer Hood, who scrambled to get to the phone on the other side of his desk.

"Ooo who's that?" I gasped, fully amused. Officer Kelly sent me a 'go to Hell' look and I smiled at her.

"Shut the hell up! You sit down and keep your mouth shut!" Officer Hood yelled at me and I couldn't help but chuckle at him. Such a small, defensive little guy. He dialed the woman's number on the phone and put it on speaker so we all could hear.

"Lia Martin Management, how may I help you?" A feminine voice came from the speaker and I smiled at Officer Hood.

"Hi Lia, this is Officer Nathan Hood of the Los Angeles police department and I'm calling to inform you that we have some new information on Kaili Taylor's case," he spoke professionally. I let out a belly laugh and held the bars for support.

"Geez, Grandpa. You sound so proper. She's not The Queen," I laughed harder and Officer Kelly looked at me with sharp eyes. *Bitch*.

"I'm sorry, I couldn't hear you clearly. Did you say 'Kaili Taylor'?" The woman's voice who I could only assume was Lia's bounced off the concrete walls.

"Yes ma'am. Anthony Ross has given us some new information that I'm sure would benefit Miss Taylor's case. If we could have you bring Miss Taylor down to the police station, we'd like to show her the security footage," Officer Kelly looked down at her shoes as she spoke, kicking globs of dirt around that had been stuck to the bottom.

"Kaili is still pretty upset from everything that's happened today. Let me speak with Mark and I'll call you back in a minute."

After Lia spoke, they said their goodbyes and hung up. Officer Kelly ran her hands over her hair and took a deep breath. She looked at me with her hands clasped together on her head.

"How can someone be so cruel? I mean I get that she broke your heart but this is borderline insanity!" She waved her hands around, walking back and forth and I watched her feet. They pointed inward when she walked. I wonder if mine do that too. I think they do. I don't know.

"Did you just decide one day 'Hey, I'm going to ruin some lives today'? Have you done this before?" She approached the metal door and leaned forward, meeting my eyes with hers.

"Don't try and get into my mind, sweetheart. You won't like it," I promised her and she let out a

174

huff. *She's so dramatic.* She stepped back and took a seat behind the desk.

"So what's for dinner?" I asked as my stomach started growling. Officer Hood stood in front of the desk, wide eyed and dumbfounded.

"Hey, Princess? Yeah, hi. Can I get something to eat or are you just gonna stand there all slack-jawed?" I mocked. He wasn't amused with my charm. Neither was Officer Kelly. She was just about to say something when the door opened.

Another officer guided a man with his hands cuffed behind his back into the cell with me. The man looked stoned and I'd be lying if I said I wasn't jealous. He plopped down on the bench and looked up at me.

"There's your sexy lady, Ross," *Officer Asshole* smiled and crossed his arms. Just as I turned to look at the man behind me, he puked all over the floor. *Awesome.*

"Hey, you're that guy that kidnapped what-his-face's sister! I saw your mugshot on the news this morning!" He wiped his mouth and ran his tongue over his yellow stained teeth. I gagged and tried to hold my breath.

"Don't talk to me," I snapped, scooting as close as I could towards the door.

"How'd you get away with it for so long? What was it, six years?" He smiled and sniffled before hacking. He spit into his pile of vomit on the floor before looking back up at me.

"*Eight*. It was *eight* years. And I didn't have to do anything to get away with it. I just did."

I don't really know why I'm talking to him, but I guess he's better company than the grumpy people on the other side of the metal bars. *Sargent Sassy* over there is still mad at me for being difficult and *Officer Asshole* is smirking at me like this whole ordeal is amusing to him. I'm sure it is. *Dick.*

"I just don't get it. Because of you, Kaili will never have a normal life and neither will Mark. You ruined her. You completely crumbled her up and threw her away. And the woman you supposedly love took her own life because of what you did. I just... I've got to get away from you. You're an evil son of a bitch, Ross, and I'll be damned if you ever see daylight again after this is all over."

Officer Kelly kept her finger pointed at me while she made her cute little speech before she stormed out of the room like a child.

"She's mean," the guy spoke behind me. The smell of his vomit was starting to make me sick.

Officer Hood adjusted his belt and stretched his shoulders. His face held a smirk and I wanted to smack it off so bad.

"Yeah, but she's kinda hot though."

# thirty
## Lia

*Unbelievable.* Two hours after the most emotional court hearing I've been through, the police find something else to charge him with. *What more could he have done?*

Kaili had already went to take a shower and I knew she didn't have any business going down to that police station. Not now, anyway. Mark and I need to do that.

I walked back into Mark's hotel room and saw him sitting with Tanner on the couch, playing some stupid video game they were obsessed with. I grabbed Mark's ear and pulled it, making him squeal and jump off the couch.

"What, Lia?" He protested loudly. I shushed him and pulled him behind me out the door and onto the balcony.

"What was that for?" He yelled. We were all a little on-edge still so I didn't hold his attitude against him. He gripped his earlobe in his fingers and growled at me like a five-year-old.

"The police station called. Apparently Anthony Ross told them something that we need to know about. They want us to come down there and watch a security tape," I told him, keeping my eye on the door to make sure Kaili wasn't anywhere near. His eyes widened and he looked around.

"Right now?" He asked.

"Yeah, kind of. I guess it's a pretty big deal," I nodded and ran a hand over my face. He sighed and looked out over the city for a second before looking back at me.

"What about Kaili?" He bit at his fingernails as he asked this and I slapped his hand out of his mouth.

"Just tell her we're going out for a bit. I'll tell Tanner to stay with her. They'll be fine," I suggested.

Mark didn't seem too thrilled about leaving her here, but that's too damn bad. He looked up at the stars for a second before covering his face with his hands.

"Whatever it is they want us down there for, it must be pretty important or else they wouldn't call us this late. Especially after we had court today," I told him, trying to persuade him.

"Alright, let's go," he finally agreed like he actually had a choice.

He helped Kaili get into bed and apply her ointment to her healing wounds. They looked a hundred times better than they did the day I first met her, but they still looked rough. Her back was the worst part, but she says she can't feel it. The only part she can feel is the tape pulling where Mark puts the bandage. Her tissue is ripped all the way across the small of her back and the skin is slowly molding back together. Her legs are almost completely healed, which makes us all happy.

She made herself comfortable and Mark sat down beside her.

"Lia and I have to go do something real quick but we'll be back soon, okay? Just call me or text me if you need me. Tanner's here, too," he told her and she nodded her head. He kissed her head and we left the room to let Tanner know what was happening.

"I hate not telling her where we're going," Mark told me once we were in my car.

"I do too. If whatever this is is really important or really bad, we'll tell her. But if it's something stupid, we won't," I reasoned with him and he agreed by nodding his head and clicking his seatbelt in place. I buckled my seatbelt as well and we rode all the way to the station in silence.

# thirty-one
## Tanner

Mark and Lia just left and I feel like it's the perfect time to tell Kaili what I'm feeling.

I knocked on her suite door and heard a faint, "Come in." Slowly opening the door, I tugged at the end of my long-sleeved shirt to make sure it was straight. She's seen me shirtless so it seemed pointless, but I still wanted to look okay.

"Hey," my voice wavered. I sounded nervous all the sudden and I could tell she noticed.

"Hey, Tanner," she smiled and tried to sit up. She winced and tensed her back, so I grabbed her arm and helped her sit up. I put her pillow behind her back and she thanked me.

"I'm tired of this stupid bandage," she giggled. *Her giggle is so cute.* She smiled up at me and I sat down in front of her.

"Kaili, I have to tell you something. Well, I don't technically *have* to, but I'm going to anyway," I started talking and she watched me with confusion littering her face.

"Okay," she kept her voice just above a whisper.

I brought my legs up in a crisscross position and held my hands in my lap. The shirt I'm wearing is in desperate need of a good washing, but I don't have time for that. I just chose to ignore the stains on it and focus on the matter at hand. I made sweater paws and twiddled my thumbs under the fabric for a few seconds before I felt her eyes staring at me.

"Just... hear me out, okay?" I asked and she nodded back. *Here goes everything.*

"These past few months, I've learned so much about you. Like, some of the things we've talked about has really opened my eyes and made me realize something. I care for you so much that it scares me sometimes.

"I don't have a small crush on you. It's so much more than that. But I know that trying to start a relationship in the middle of all this mess or complicating things with Mark is the last thing I want to do to you. You deserve better than that. So... I'm not asking you to be my girlfriend. What I'm asking is that you allow me to be your protector."

The words spilled out of my mouth before I could process them and I felt just as surprised as Kaili looked when I finished. She blinked her eyes a few times and I held tighter to my sweater paws. I subconsciously bit my lip and she tilted her head to the side.

"My protector? What does that mean? Like, I know what the word means, but what do you mean?" She asked.

I licked my chapped lips and thought for a bit. I couldn't gage what her emotion was, but I knew she felt *something*. Shaking my hands out of my sleeves and lacing my fingers together, I answered her.

"I want to be there for you. I want to be the one you run to when you're scared. I don't want you to be scared or anything, but you get my point, right? I want to be that for you. I want to be your comfort because you're that for me and I don't think you realize it.

"But you've just went through an insanely chaotic event in your life and I don't want to make it any harder on you by making you question how I feel towards you. Does any of that even make sense? I feel like it doesn't."

She was smiling as I spoke. I'm guessing she found my nervousness amusing. I'm sure it was.

"It makes sense. I guess you didn't realize that you already are my protector," she spoke so quietly at the end, I almost missed it.

"When I saw you in Bradley's face on the TV, I wasn't thinking about Anthony Ross. I was thinking about when you told me you fought people after your brother passed. I don't like seeing that side of you."

She's right. That's exactly how I was when Allen died. I was violent and mean and I hated myself.

I looked up at her and she had her eyes focused elsewhere. I pulled my phone out of my pocket and went into my music library, searching for the song I wanted to show her. The album art showed on my screen and I tapped the album picture with my thumb.

"This should be our song," I told her, pressing play.

"What is it?" She asked me, furrowing her eyebrows together. I looked up at her and smiled, turning the volume up a little more. The music started and I bobbed my head along with the beat.

"Just listen," I spoke over the music before the first verse was sang.

Kaili listened closely to the lyrics and I watched her facial expressions. She went from interested to confused.

"I can't tell what she's saying," she spoke over the song and I paused the song.

"It's about enemy fire which is like all the bad things in the world and she's saying she wants a soldier to protect her from it. Stuff like Anthony Ross, Bradley Michaels, and Allen's cancer for example. You're my soldier as I'm yours."

She nodded her head and smiled down at her legs. I hope I'm the reason for that smile. Unless she's genuinely happy that she has legs. I mean I guess it's pretty rad that she has legs, but I don't know why she'd pick now to be excited about it.

"I like it," she spoke up and I flinched, not exactly prepared for her to talk. I felt my cheeks blush as if she could hear my thoughts.

"Me too," I smiled over at her. She moved a little and groaned. I can't imagine the pain she's went through.

"Are you okay?" I asked her.

"If you ask me that one more time, I'm going to hurt you," she grumbled and smiled. I laughed at her threat and helped her get comfortable.

"Thank you," she smiled at me. I stuck my tongue out at her and she laughed. I pressed play on the song again and laid back on her bed with my head on her lap and her fingers messing with my hair.

# thirty-two
## Mark

I hadn't noticed it before but the police station is oddly quiet and creepy on the outside. And the fact that it was getting dark didn't help at all. We walked inside and Officer Craig took us back to the interrogation room Kaili was in when she was questioned. He showed us to some chairs and we both sat down.

"What's this all about?" Lia asked quite sharply. Officer Craig held up his hand and opened the door. He waved to someone we couldn't see and they walked up to the door. I recognized her as Officer Kelly when she walked in.

"Hi guys. I'm sorry we called so late, but Mister Ross has revealed something disturbing to us that we thought you'd want to know about," she spoke, keeping her hands clasped together.

"Does it have anything to do with Kaili or Mark? Because if not, then there's no reason for you to call us this late," Lia raised her voice. Her snappy attitude was becoming childish, but I bit my tongue. She's like a mother to me in a way that I'm afraid to back-sass her in fear of getting my ears pinched.

"Yes ma'am, it does. Now, Mark, by any chance were your parents' names Emily and Jason?"

The question caught me by surprise. I've never mentioned my parents' names in interviews or on any kind of social media. I doubt Lia even knew what their names were. Sure, the police have access to literally *everything*, but something about the tone in her voice got my attention.

"H… How did you know that?" I stumbled over my words.

Officer Kelly turned on the small computer monitor and clicked on a few things before a security camera shot came up on the screen of Anthony Ross and another police officer. She pressed a button and the image started moving.

I watched in awe and felt my anger growing by the second.

"The last time someone stole the love of my life from me, I stalked them and kidnapped their daughter."

That sentence fueled a fire I didn't know could be started inside me. His voice was ringing in my ears as he told the officers more and more. My vision was getting blurry and the palms of my hands were being assaulted by my finger nails.

"I knew exactly who I was kidnapping when I took Kaili…"

I leaned closer to the screen and tried not to pick it up and throw it against the wall.

"Her mom, Emily, was the love of my life…"

*Mom? He knew Mom?*

"…but she left me for another man. Kaili's dad."

*DAD KNEW HIM?*

My palms were aching and my leg wouldn't stop bouncing up and down. Lia touched my shoulder and I shrugged her off. The last thing I want is to be touched right now. No, the last thing I want is to hear this bastard talk about my family any more.

"I took a bunch of her stuff she threw away when she moved in with Jason and kept it in the basement where I had Kaili."

*Breathe, Mark.*

"So Kaili was surrounded by her mom's stuff the whole time and had no idea."

My vision went red. I jumped out of my chair and lost control completely. All I could hear was a mixture of Anthony Ross's voice and my blood pounding in my ears. My fist hit the wall and I looked away from the hole I made. I grabbed the chair I was in and slammed it against the floor.

"MARK! STOP IT!"

Before I knew it, two men held my shoulders and arms in place and Lia had my face cupped in her hands.

"Mark, breathe," she pleaded with me and I shook out of the men's hands. My hands went to my hair and I tugged at my scalp, trying to calm down. *You know what, forget being calm.*

"I want him dead," I growled.

My voice was deeper than I expected and Officer Kelly gawked at my words. All I could see was a blurry mess and some drywall on the floor.

"Mark, calm down. He's going to prison. It's okay," Lia tried her best to defuse my inner bomb, but

186

it wasn't working. I paced around the room and tried to keep my hands to myself.

"No it's not! That man has completely ruined our lives and I want him dead. I don't care if I have to kill him myself, I want him dead. He deserves to die for what he's done to my family, Lia," I yelled back at her and she took a few steps backwards.

"Mister Taylor, please sit down," Officer Kelly grabbed my shoulder. I quickly jerked out of her hold and stormed out of the room.

I got halfway down the hallway and punched another wall. All I felt was anger. My knuckles were bruising, but I didn't care. I pulled at my hair and leaned against the wall before slowly sinking down it. My butt hit the floor and I pulled my knees to my chest.

I sat alone for a minute before Lia sat down beside me. She sank down the wall like I did and let out a sigh.

"I want him dead, Lia," I whispered to her. My throat was sore from all the crying and screaming I hadn't realize I'd done. She put a hand on my back and rubbed it in circles.

"I know you do. He's going to spend the rest of his life in prison. He will die eventually." Her voice was motherly and I tried my best to keep in my emotions. I hadn't done such a hot job of that today to be honest.

"He had everything planned out. He watched us for years and just… Just… And now she's pregnant and I don't know what to do. I can't fix this."

My emotions brutally knocked down my brick wall and I began sobbing. Lia stopped rubbing my back and laid her arm across me and held me. She stayed quiet while I cried and just held me together. Her being here for me made me miss my mom even more and I hate knowing that Anthony Ross is part of the reason she's gone.

Lia patted my back and I raised up, wiping my eyes and looking at the wall in front of me.

"Tell me how to fix this," I begged quietly. Lia stretched her legs out and crossed her ankles. Her chest rose in a deep breath and I felt my chin quivering. *I hate Anthony Ross.* No person in this world has ever made me feel as helpless as this man has.

"I don't know how to fix it, but I think it would be best to cancel the rest of this tour. Just take Kaili home for a few months and relax, ya know? You both need it."

Her suggestion knocked the wind out of me. I know she's right. I just wish canceling the tour wasn't our best option. I have yet to cancel a show, much less an entire half of a tour. I don't want to let my fans down. They are my entire existence. If it wasn't for them, I don't think I'd be alive today.

"How am I supposed to tell her?" I asked.

"Don't. She doesn't have to know about this. Any of this," she suggested. She grabbed onto my shoulder and shook me a bit. I pondered her words and shook my head.

"She deserves to know why he did it," I argued.

I hate it when people keep things from me, and it just feels wrong to do it to Kaili. She deserves better than that. She deserves a better brother. I'm a shitty one.

My mind was a jumbled mess; a mixture of started thoughts that were never finished. Every thought I had was washed away with the current. The only way out of this whole thing is to listen to Lia and let her handle it.

She kept quiet as an officer stepped around us to walk down the hallway. When she finally did speak, all she said was, "let's go". I stood up and offered my hand to her, which she happily took. Officer Kelly came out into the hallway and stood before us with a large manila envelope in her hand.

"Here's a copy of the footage and some paperwork for you to take to Kaili. Considering the circumstances, we won't charge you for punching the walls and acting out like you did. Just don't tell anyone about that and you won't hear about it from us."

Officer Kelly handed me the envelope and offered me a smile before turning and walking away. I didn't get a chance to apologize for my behavior, but I believe it was justified. I tucked the envelope under my arm and we started to leave when one of the officers who tried to contain me earlier stepped in front of us.

"There are paparazzi across the street waiting for you. If you want one of us to go get your vehicle, we'll bring it around the back and sneak you out that way." He seemed intimidated by me, which I would have laughed at if I wasn't so angry. Not only with Anthony Ross, but with myself for acting like a child.

I huffed at the mention of the paps. They're literally everywhere. I honestly don't know how they find me all the time but they do. *Every time*. They especially seem to catch me when I'm with Natalie, who I miss dearly. I wish she'd hurry up and come back to California, but I know she's busy. I'm so proud of her, but I'm afraid that she will find someone better for her.

Lia handed over her keys and we waited while the officer retrieved her car. Once we climbed into her car to leave, I sank down into my seat and pulled my hood up on my head. She kept one hand on the wheel and started digging through her purse with the other.

"Here."

In her hand was a prescription bottle I was way too familiar with. She handed me my anxiety pills and grabbed her drink. I took the bottle from her and looked at it. These things have been my security blanket for two years and I'm tired of them.

"No," I fumed, handing them back to her.

"Mark, you need to take them. They'll help you," she tried to hand them back to me. I refused and crossed my arms.

"I don't want them. Kaili didn't have anxiety pills when she was fighting for her life in a psychopath's basement. I'm done taking them," I declared and Lia dropped the bottle back in her purse. I noticed a small smile playing on her lips and she finally looked over at me.

"You're a stubborn little shit, you know that?" She pointed out. I couldn't help but smile at her words and try to sink farther into my seat.

# thirty-three

## Kaili

"Come on, this is the best song ever created!"

Tanner was lying beside me on my bed with his phone playing a song. He had been playing it over and over for the last twenty minutes just to prove a point, which he wasn't doing. His point was pointless.

"It's horrible! There's no words!" I replied, trying not to laugh at how defensive he was getting.

"Yeah, no words to describe how amazing it is!" He yelled back with humor seeping out with the words.

He turned the volume up louder and started making the beat on his stomach with his hands. Unimaginable noises were coming from his lips and he bobbed his head along with the sounds he was making. He threw his arms around in an intense part of the song and ended up hitting his hand on the headboard.

My stomach hurt from laughing so much and his phone started ringing.

"It's Maaaark," he sang, swiping his thumb across the screen.

"Hey man, what's up?" He answered the phone and started poking and pulling at the blanket under us.

He touched the speaker button and Mark's voice bounced off the walls.

"Hey, is Kaili with you?" I could hear defeat in his voice and it worried me, but I tried not to show it. Tanner slung his hurt hand around and pouted while I smiled at him.

"Yeah, I'm here," I spoke up. Tanner looked over at me with his eyebrows pushed together and I scrunched my nose at him. We both giggled quietly.

"We need to have a team meeting when Lia and I get back. We're bringing home pizza, too, so don't eat anything yet," he spoke. We heard a car horn in the background and I nodded my head before realizing he couldn't see me.

"Is everything okay?" Tanner asked into the phone. My fingers started pulling on loose strings at the bottom of my shirt and I had to stop myself from pulling them out. Mark sighed on his end of the phone and I frowned.

"No, not really. But it will be. I'll see you in a bit, okay? Love you guys." And with that, he hung up the phone. Tanner's music started playing again and he paused it.

"What do you think is going on?" I asked him. He sat up and looked back at me with a straight face.

"Enemy fire," he whispered and I couldn't help but let out a laugh.

He helped me get out of bed and I followed him down the hall that leads to the suite living room. He skipped down the hallway and stopped when he saw I was moving slower than him. Like a true protector would, he came back and helped me walk down the hall and sit on the couch. Within a few minutes, Mark and Lia returned with pizza in hand.

# thirty-four
## Kaili

The air felt tense as we ate but I didn't want to be the one to start the conversation. Lia stayed pretty quiet, commenting only on the taste of the pizza being "inadequate". I didn't know what that meant, but didn't feel like asking.

Mark threw a piece of crust back in the box and laid back, sticking his stomach out dramatically.

"Damn, that was good," he muttered.

"Mark…" Lia got onto him for using the bad word. She reminds me so much of Mom, which makes me miss her even more. If only I could have had one more day with her; with both my parents. If I end up being half the woman my mother was, my baby is going to have a wonderful mommy.

Tanner cleared his throat loudly and Mark sat up straight.

"Alright, let's just get to it. When we left earlier, we didn't tell you where we were going. Only because we didn't know why we were going in the first place," Lia started, looking back and forth between Tanner and me. I immediately regretted not grabbing my sweatshirt on the way out of my room. Since I didn't have it, I was left with my shirt hem to mess with.

Lia reached across the coffee table and touched my leg and my thoughts flashed to Anthony Ross. His hands were hard and rough and I hated them. Instinctively, I jerked my leg away from her and she frowned.

"I'm sorry, dear," she apologized and I held my eyes shut.

"It's okay. I just... I didn't know you were gonna do that..." I didn't want to tell her where my mind went and technically I wasn't lying. I didn't know she was going to touch me.

She gave me a knowing smile and brought her hands back to her lap as she spoke again. She puts off such a hard vibe to everyone else but she's actually one of the sweetest people I know. Not that I know that many people, but still.

"The police called us down to the station. They wanted to talk to you, actually, but Mark and I decided that you didn't need to go anywhere else today after that court hearing. That was stressful enough for all of us," Lia started. She kept her hands in her lap as she spoke to me. I looked over at Mark and he was already looking at me. He does that a lot. He looks at me first before I look at him. Maybe it's just a Mark thing.

"What did they want?" I questioned. Tanner leaned back on me and laid his head on my folded legs. He smiled up at me, making me blush and he stuck his tongue out in a childish way. *He's such a goofball*. My hand landed on his chest and he faked a painful grunt.

"Well, he told them something. He... He and Mom dated before she met Dad," Mark spoke slowly. I looked at him and he had his bottom lip between his teeth.

"What? He knew Mom?" My heart was pounding hard and my head was throbbing. I wanted to deny it so bad, but a part of me knew he wasn't kidding. *This can't be true.* He nodded at me and I swear my jaw fell off and rolled under the couch.

"Security footage in the holding cell showed him telling a police officer that he loved a woman. Your mom. And he said that your dad took her away from him and he wanted revenge. So he followed you guys everywhere and planned everything out. He knew who you were before he took you, Kaili. He knew the whole time. And according to him, all the stuff in the basement was your mother's."

Lia's voice seemed to get quieter and quieter as my heart beat out of my chest. I couldn't breathe. My stomach was tight. My head hurt. Even my eyes hurt from squeezing my eyelids shut on them. Everything from the top of my head to the pit of my stomach felt like it was burning and I desperately wanted the pain to go away.

Tanner sat up and held onto my hand while the information registered. All the clothes I wore. All those boxes. The dresser I destroyed with the tally marks. The mirror. All of it was Mom's. The woman who killed herself because she was so depressed about me being gone and Dad being killed.

*DAD!*

*He knew Anthony Ross. Mom knew Anthony Ross. He knew us.*

All these thoughts were way too much.

"Kaili," Mark's voice broke right through me as he stood in front of me. He pulled me off the couch and held me tight against his body.

I completely let go of every emotion I tried to hide for the past few months. I screamed. I cried. I cursed out loud. Every little piece of my heart was burning inside of me.

His arms seemed to get tighter around me as I screamed. While the gesture was comforting, I still felt trapped. Trapped in this crazy, messed up story that should have never been written. Just when I think I'm getting my happy ending, there's something else to screw it up.

I should have known there was some story behind the mirror and the clothes. Anthony Ross couldn't have been married or had kids because his voice was the only voice I heard for the past eight years. I just thought the stuff in the basement was left by the last family that lived there. Or maybe they were his mom's things. I never expected it to be Mom's stuff.

What did Mark and I do to deserve this? We did nothing. We didn't know Anthony Ross existed when we were younger. I didn't steal Mom away from him. I didn't break his heart. It's not my fault Mom left him for Dad.

I decided right that second that I needed to get her things. *Those are my momma's things, not his. He can't have them any longer.* My words were out before I could really think about what I was saying.

"I want to get Mom's stuff."

I'm not sure who I surprised more with that declaration; Lia, Tanner, or Mark. All three of them were wide eyed. Mark let me go and looked into my eyes with worry. Every part of me was being ripped apart and I hated that he felt it too.

"I don't think that's such a good idea sweetie..." Lia touched my back. I moved around her and backed away, shaking my head.

"No. I need to get Mom's stuff. It's hers. I can't leave it there." My back hit the wall and I leaned against it. Lia came towards me and held her arms out, offering a hug. I gladly accepted and her hands held my back and the back of my head in the most comforting way. Tanner's eyes never left my face.

"I'll call Officer Kelly in the morning and we'll see if we can go get your stuff. Shh. It's okay," Lia promised me. My fingers gripped her shirt and I cried on her shoulder. She held me together while my world collapsed around me for the millionth time.

# thirty-five
## Mark

Officer Kelly told Lia she would take us to Anthony Ross' house. It's being repossessed tomorrow, so all of his things have to be moved out today anyway. While the police department and a few volunteer fireman are working on cleaning out the house, we're allowed to take anything we want from the basement.

But before we can go to his house, Kaili has to take an anxiety test at the police station. It consists of a therapist asking her questions and showing her pictures to see what triggers her anxiety. *What else could trigger her anxiety other than things that remind her of Anthony Ross? Duh.* I swear, these people get paid way too much to do a simple job.

Once her test was over and the therapist gave her a prescription for anxiety pills, we left with Officer Kelly. Kaili held the prescription in her hands and crumpled up the paper.

"What are you doing?" I asked her. She handed me the ball of paper and shrugged.

"You guys are my anxiety medicine," she spoke, pointing to Tanner, then Lia, then me. She made sweater paws and held her hands in her lap with a small smile on her face.

"I used to be on anxiety pills, but I quit taking them because I felt guilty." Officer Kelly made a right turn down Rose Street as I spoke.

"Guilty about what?" Kaili looked over at me and pushed her hair out of her face with her arm.

"I felt guilty because my anxiety was nothing compared to what you went through and I felt like a baby. So I quit taking them. I don't need them anymore, anyway. Not now that you've been rescued," I revealed to her. It felt good talking to my sister about this. She and I have more in common than most people think.

"Just because I went through something terrible doesn't make your anxiety any less of a problem. People handle different things in different ways. It doesn't make anyone better or worse than you or make you a baby," she pulled on a string from her jeans as she spoke.

*Hmm.*

I thought about what she said while watching out the window as we drove through Los Angeles. This city has been my home for such a long time. Although my house is in Atlanta, LA is where it all started. My dreams brought me out here and God's grace got me to where I am today.

Tanner and Lia both live with me but in their own separate sections of my house. *Okay, mansion. Whatever.* It's a picture perfect house for a young guy like myself but it doesn't feel like home. There's nothing sentimental from my parents or grandparents in that house. The only thing with sentimental value I have in there is my first guitar I bought myself and my award collection in the glass case in the safe.

"This is it," Officer Kelly pulled into a driveway and parked the car. I think I might have caught whiplash from being ripped out of my thoughts that quickly. It gave me a headache. I looked over and noticed Kaili fidgeting with the bottom hem of her sweatshirt; an anxious habit that we both have.

I'm not sure what I was expecting when we pulled up to Anthony Ross' house, but a lawn gnome with a bright pink hat sitting in a flower bed wasn't on the list. The place looked normal on the outside and I was terrified to see the inside.

There was a large dumpster already half full of junk and broken furniture sitting in the yard. Men and women were moving about, carrying different things to the dumpster. They paid no attention to us, which was nice considering how much attention I usually get. It's nice to be treated like a normal guy every once in a while.

Two firemen were carrying a mattress out when we got out of the car. One of them noticed us and gestured towards us with his head.

"Can I help you folks?" The man spoke up and dropped his end of the mattress on the grass.

"Yes. I've brought Kaili Taylor and her family here to see the basement," Officer Kelly gestured towards us and Kaili stood with half her body hidden behind me.

"Whoa. *The* Kaili Taylor? You're her?" The man's eyes grew wide and he pulled his gloves off his hands. He looked at Kaili and she moved out from her hiding place.

"Sweetheart, you are lucky to be alive right now. A few of the guys and I went in the basement earlier just to look around and that place is scary. We didn't touch anythin', so it should be just the same as the last time you seen it," the man spoke with a thick southern accent. Kaili just nodded at him and he offered his hand for her to shake. She slowly shook it and he excused himself to finish his job.

Kaili looked back at me and I grabbed ahold of her hand.

"Are you ready?" I asked her, watching as she looked around in the yard. I knew she was afraid that if she spoke she'd cry, so I held tighter to her hand and followed Officer Kelly into the house.

There was a dark, narrow hallway directly in front of us and a kitchen area to the right as we walk in the front door. We stepped inside and Officer Kelly asked a volunteer where the basement was.

"One... Two..." Kaili started whispering numbers and grabbed my arm with her free hand.

"What are you counting?" I whispered to her. She looked up in front of us and gasped.

Down the narrow hallway in front of us was a closed door. "Three... Four... Five..." I counted with her as we stepped forward. With every number voiced and every step taken, her grip on my arm tightened. I held onto her, too, afraid that if I were to let go she'd run away.

When we got to "eight", I looked behind us at Tanner. He was looking away from us and Lia was nowhere to be seen. Officer Kelly knocked on the basement door and waited to see if anyone was down there. No sound came, so she placed her hand on the knob before looking back at Kaili.

"Are you ready?" She raised an eyebrow. Kaili nodded her head and leaned closer to me. Just as she was about to open the basement door, Officer Kelly looked behind us.

"Hey bud!" Kaili flinched and closed her eyes and I turned to see who Officer Kelly was talking to. Andrew trotted down the hall and I shook his hand.

"Hi Kaili," he offered her a huge grin and she smiled weakly at him.

"Who's this?" Lia and Tanner walked up and asked at the same time.

"This is my brother, Andrew. He's the man who found Kaili in there," Officer Kelly beat me to the explanation.

"He's your brother?" Kaili asked. I definitely didn't see that coming, but they do look very similar.

"Yep. Small world, huh?" Andrew smiled at my sister and looked behind us at the door.

"Have you guys went down there yet?" He nodded his head towards the door. Kaili shook her head and shifted her weight from one foot to the other.

"No. We were just about to," I told him. Officer Kelly grabbed the doorknob again and Kaili took a deep breath. As the door creaked open, I pulled my baby sister closer to me. Officer Kelly led the way and walked down the steps and Kaili stood on the top step, motionless.

"Will you carry me down? I don't trust my legs going down the stairs," she asked me and I nodded.

"I got it," Tanner interjected and stepped down two stairs in front of her.

Tanner and I had a serious talk this morning about his intentions with my sister and he made it very clear that he wasn't looking to hurt her. He said he wanted to be her "protector", to which I brought up his fear of spiders and jokingly called him a pussy. But I will say I'm happy that they get along so well. Most importantly, I'm glad he's someone Kaili can confide in.

"Help her get on my back, Mark." He hunched over and I did as he requested. She held tight to his shoulders and his hands latched onto the back of her knees. It means the world to me that my best friend cares for my sister so much.

I walked down ahead of them and jumped off the last step. When I looked back, Kaili had her eyes hidden behind Tanner's shoulder. Her little fingers were wrapped around her arms and she was sniffling. When Tanner put her on her feet, I could see the tears falling from her eyes.

Looking around, I felt like I finally understood. The room was dark and smelt like death. The floor was clear of trash, but there were boxes piled up along the back wall. The mirror Anthony Ross mentioned in the security tape was propped up against some boxes.

The rusted pipes along the ceiling were dripping into different things on the floor. There were buckets, hats, and what looked like dresser drawers filling with water as the slow dripping continued. A bag of moldy bread was laying on a box and I shook my head.

This place is terrible. Worse than that. This place is absolute *Hell*. I can't believe I'm in the exact same place that Kaili lived in for all these years. Just looking at the place broke my heart.

I heard what sounded like wood splitting and turned around. Tanner had his hands on two pieces of wood that covered the only window. He pulled hard, but couldn't get them to move. I looked away from him and saw Kaili standing under the stairs with her hands on top of a wooden desk. She held what looked like a razor blade between her fingers and I walked to her cautiously.

"This desk was Mom's and I ruined it," she spoke, her voice just above a whisper. When I looked at the desk, my chest tightened. The surface was covered in tally marks.

"Maybe not. It might not have been Mom's. It might have actually been his," I tried to reassure both of us. We probably won't ever know if it was Mom's or not, but that's okay.

My fingers ran over the surface and I started counting the tallies.

"There's 98," Kaili interrupted my counting.

"They helped me remember how long I was down here. The last day made 98 months," she continued. The blade in her hand moved around in her fingers and she gripped it tightly. She hunched over and began carving into the wood.

In the bottom right corner of the desk top, she carved *FREE* into the surface before tossing the blade onto it and stepping back. When she finally looked up at me, I could see the pieces of my sister finally falling back together in a messy masterpiece.

# thirty-six
## Kaili

Nobody understands how many horrifying memories this place brings back. The entire room is one big rut in my life. Every inch of this room is haunting. The walls, the ceiling, the stairs, everything. Every piece of it is part of the reason I am the way I am.

Tanner and Mark started sorting through the boxes as I walked around the basement. I wouldn't call it reminiscing, but that's the only way I can explain what I was doing.

Every time someone would walk up the stairs, I could see Anthony Ross doing the same but in an orange jumpsuit and his wrists in hand cuffs behind his back. When someone walked into the front door upstairs, I counted their steps. When you've done the same things for eight years, they become an instinct that you can't shake.

"Kaili?"

I turned around and Tanner was standing behind me with a box in his hands.

"Yeah?" I asked. He dipped his head down and frowned.

"Are you alright? You spaced out," he replied. I looked around the room for a second and smiled.

"Yeah, I'm alright. Just a lot of memories down here," I told him. His presence made this experience a whole lot easier for me.

"Ya know, you're braver than you think you are, kiddo," he complimented as he placed the box aside and grabbed a blanket the firemen provided to lay on the floor. He laid it down and brushed his hands off on his shorts.

"How?" We sat down on the blanket and he opened up the box. Inside was a bunch of old clothes that I'd worn over the years and washed the best I could in my drip buckets.

"Just coming back here is brave. I know you didn't come back just for your mom's stuff." He pulled a shirt out and looked at the worn material. I smiled, remembering it to be my favorite shirt from here.

"I wanted to see the place one last time. I might need pancake therapy after this, but it's worth it," I admitted to him, making him smile.

"I think that can be arranged," he chuckled.

"Hey guys." Mark sat down beside me and put his arm around my shoulder.

"I found a dead snake in one of the boxes. It was super gross," he continued. He made a disgusted face and I couldn't help but laugh.

"Now you see what I had to deal with for all those years," I joked. I was trying to make light of the situation, but Mark just sighed and smashed his lips together.

"How did you live down here?" He asked, taking out a shirt and crinkling his nose at the stains all over it.

"I don't know. I just did. He gave me a bag of bread once a month and I used those buckets and stuff to get water to drink," I told them. I thought back to one time when the water was shut off for a few days and I had to try to save all I had.

"Where did you go to the bathroom?" Tanner looked around for any signs of a toilet and I pointed to the drain on the floor across the room.

"Seriously? That's horrible," he shook his head and I shrugged my shoulders.

"It's all I had," I spoke. My fingers ran over my wrists and I took a deep breath.

# thirty-seven
## Mark

A few firemen offered to take the stuff up and load it into a moving truck Lia had rented for us. Tanner and I could have easily done it ourselves, but neither one of us wanted to leave Kaili's side.

Her and I sorted through more of Mom's stuff and ended up finding the clothes Kaili was wearing the day she was kidnapped. The colors were faded and the material was ripped in several places.

"These probably still fit me," she observed as she held the shorts up to her waist.

"Probably. You need to get some meat on them bones, squirt," I laughed heartedly and she smiled at me, tossing the shorts in my face.

Once the last box was loaded, Kaili looked around the empty basement. She looked up at the ceiling and her face broke into a small frown.

"I spent so many days just laying down here feeling completely alone. I had no idea I was with Mom's stuff the whole time. I just can't seem to wrap my head around that."

I slung my arm over her shoulder and she leaned her head on me. I heard her sniffle and I squeezed her arm.

"Why me?" The tone in her voice was enough to make even the toughest man's heart break.

"I mean, I know everything happens for a reason, but why me? Why you? What did we do to deserve this? Why did Mom have to make a crazy man fall in love with her?" My lip quivered as she spoke and I managed to swallow the lump in my throat.

"I wish I knew the answer to that. I really do. All I know is that God has had His hand on us this whole time."

She looked over at me with tears in her eyes.

"I just... I feel like I've ruined your life. If I would have just died in here, you wouldn't have to cancel your tour or take care of me all the time. I'm a burden and I hate it."

I pulled her into my chest and shook my head violently.

"No. No you're not. Kaili, you being found is the greatest thing that's ever happened to me; better than any award or tour or any amount of money. All of that can wait, but you're my baby sister. Please don't ever feel like a burden."

I hated hearing her say that. There's no way in hell she could be a burden to me. With her back in my life, the tour is what's burdening me.

"Tomorrow, I'm having a meeting with the record label. Then a press release about canceling the tour. And after that, we're going to my place in Atlanta. Everything will calm down and we can relax for a bit and we can go to the beach in Florida. Or we can go to the Atlanta Aquarium. Just you and me or we can bring Tanner and Lia. Natalie can come down when she gets done working, too. Whatever you want to do, we can do it."

I tried as hard as I could to make her feel better. I want her to know she's my main priority right now. She's all I have left.

She didn't speak. All she could do was nod, which was enough.

We went outside and found Tanner and Officer Kelly loading the desk into the back of the moving truck.

"And what exactly are you planning to do with it?" Lia had her hand on her hip, looking at him with an eyebrow raised.

"I'll tell you later." He cocked his head towards us and Lia nodded in understanding.

As promised to Kaili by Tanner, we ate dinner at Hank & Dolores's. She said she was joking when she told him she needed pancake therapy, but we all know she was serious. We all needed it.

"Hey, can we stop at the hardware place on the way back to the hotel? I need to grab a few things real quick." Tanner spoke up as we ate.

"Yeah, what do you need to get?" Lia asked him. He shrugged his shoulders.

"A few things. No big deal."

If I know my best friend as well as I think I do, then I know he's up to something.

# thirty-eight
## Kaili

"Kaili! Look over here!"

"Kaili, what's your take on Bradley Michaels and the way your friend Tanner attacked him?"

"Kaili! Hey! Smile!"

"Are you and Tanner dating?"

Paparazzi were surrounding me. They followed us all the way from the hotel, which didn't really surprise me. I knew they had a job to do. I just wish they didn't have to be so aggressive while doing it.

Mark's record label building was intimidating enough without all the camera flashes. It's tall and oddly shaped. Instead of the base of the building being a square, this one is a circle. And the entire building is like a giant mirror.

The meeting with his record label is only supposed to last a few minutes while the press release will be much longer. Tanner and Lia are with us, along with the people who work on tour with him. They're here to sit in the audience during the press release while Mark and Lia make the announcement and answer questions.

Mark led us into a big room with a large table right in the middle of it. There were big black chairs all around it and one at each end.

"Where do I sit?" I asked, pulling on the sleeves of my sweatshirt. The sleeves were tied around my waist, as it was way too hot outside to wear it normally. I knew I couldn't go a day without it, so Mark showed me how to tie it around my waist before we left the hotel.

He pointed to one of the chairs and Tanner pulled it out for me. He sat down beside me and Mark sat on the other side at the head of the table. Lia sat across from me, smiling and typing away on her phone. She has a flight tomorrow morning to Washington where her parents live. I can only imagine her excitement.

Within a minute, the chairs around the table filled up with men and women all dressed in business suits. All of them shook hands with Mark and Lia, but paid no mind to me or Tanner.

"What they don't know is that my dad owns this building *and* the record company," Tanner whispered in my ear. I looked over at him and he held a goofy smile.

"Really?" I asked quietly. He nodded and ran his tongue over his bottom lip; something I have noticed he does when he's amused.

"Yeah. My dad is a landlord and owns some of the biggest buildings in LA, including this one. So needless to say, I have more money in my bank account than anyone in this room besides Mark." He kept his voice down and sent a sarcastic smile to one of the men in the room.

"Money isn't everything, you know," I whispered to him.

"To them it is."

We stopped whispering when Lia stood up and held her hands together. Mark looked over at Tanner and I and gave Tanner a weird look, then smiled and shook his head.

"Mark knows," Tanner whispered. I smiled and looked up at Lia.

"As Mark's career-long manager, I called this meeting today with all of you to talk about a few things. As all of you should know, Mark's sister Kaili was found a little than a month ago. We have been to court and spent a few days at the police station working on her case. Not only is this a huge stress on Kaili, but on all of us. She means the world to us, and we only want what's best for her.

"Now, in order for us to do everything we can to ensure Kaili and Mark are taken care of, we have decided to cancel the remainder of our world tour. Mark will be taking his sister to his Atlanta home for some much needed relaxation time. This decision is not open for negotiation or discussion. Our minds have been made up and there's absolutely nothing that could change them.

"With that said, the traveling crew will be paid for the remainder of the tour, as stated in their contracts. They will not be contacted by any media personnel, as also stated in their contracts. This includes all dancers, musicians, merchandisers, technicians, security, and etcetera.

"So, on behalf of Mark and Kaili Taylor, I hereby conclude this business meeting. Any negative opinions will be handled by Mark and Kaili's lawyer. Thank you."

Every jaw in the room except ours dropped as she spoke quickly and authoritatively.

"Come on, guys," Lia motioned for us to stand and follow her out of the room. Her strut was strong as she moved down the hall, turning the heads of the workers walking around.

"Wait so that's it? It was that easy?" Mark asked once we got in an elevator as Lia checked her hair and makeup in the mirrors lining the walls.

"No, but that was the easiest part. I did everything last night when we got to the hotel. I called every international arena you were scheduled to hit and let them know we weren't coming. I let every crew member know so they can plan vacations or go home or whatever they want while still being paid. And the only way to get the people here to listen is to not give them a chance to speak."

She ran a hand over her perfectly styled hair and turned back to us with a smile.

"Are you Lia Martin or Superwoman?" Tanner leaned against the wall as he asked the question, making us all laugh.

"Ask me again after this press conference," she giggled as the doors opened, causing her to go back into manager mode. She cleared her throat and adjusted her suit jacket as she walked towards the door.

Ten minutes and two ibuprofen pills later, we were out of the press conference.

"So, am I Superwoman or am I Superwoman?" Lia boasted quietly to me as we walked down a hallway. Every single journalist in the press conference was intimidated by her. They stayed quiet and let her talk. Not a single question was asked.

"You're definitely Superwoman," I agreed, to which she smiled and nudged me with her elbow.

"If anyone here is Superwoman it's you, girly. What do you say we go get some ice cream?" She tossed her arm around my shoulders and pulled me close to her. Mark held the door open for us as we left the building.

"Sounds like a plan to me," he told her.

As we walked to the car, Lia kept her arm over me and Dave pushed through the paparazzi to clear a path for us. As the cameras flashed, I looked up at Lia. She shouted at the cameras and used her free arm to block the paparazzi from getting pictures of me. I looked to my right and saw Tanner using his hat to block cameras from me also.

Mark was a few steps ahead of us with his face hidden by Dave. Every now and then, he'd turn to look at me and stick his tongue out. I sent him a smile in return and held tighter to Lia as her hand ran up and down my arm.

# thirty-nine
## Mark

A last minute decision by me ended up putting us in Pensacola, Florida for a week while my house is being cleaned thoroughly by professionals. Tanner will be with us for a few days, but he has to go back to Atlanta early to "take care of business", whatever that means.

I sent Dave to Atlanta to keep an eye on everything while we're here. He assured me that there was nothing to worry about and, oddly enough, I wasn't all that worried in the first place. All of my personal things were locked in a giant safe room anyway.

The moving truck is scheduled to get to my place in two days, so we'll have plenty to do when we get back. I'm excited and nervous for Kaili to see my home. Well, it's not really *home*, but it's mine. With her there, maybe it will feel more like a home.

Kaili, Tanner, and I flew down this morning and had a car brought to the airport. She was afraid of flying, so I stayed awake with her and helped her through it. Jet lag threatened to take me down a few times but I prevailed.

Once we got to our hotel, Tanner headed for the gym while Kaili and I decided to go down to the beach. I made a few phone calls on the way down and eventually found out about a closed off portion of the beach that we could go to. Being famous has its perks.

At the beach, I felt like we were both relaxed. The water moved back and forth over our bare feet and Kaili dug her toes in the sand. We sat down beside each other and looked out over the ocean.

"It's amazing out here," she smiled at the small crab crawling towards the water. The crab raised his claws at her and she let out a faint giggle.

"It's crazy to think that this is two worlds coming together. Like right where the edge of the water meets the dry sand. Do you know what I mean?" She looked up at me as she asked. I nodded and brought my knees up under my chin.

"The ocean is a whole different world. There's parts of it humans haven't seen and probably won't ever see," I told her, looking out at the waves. She nodded and looked back at the crab. It walked faster towards the water and eventually got swept up by a wave.

"I wish Mom and Dad were here," I thought out loud. She sighed and brought her knees up like mine. She laid her arms across them and looked over at me.

"Me too," she frowned.

I thought about when we were little and Mom and Dad took us to a beach in Japan across town from the base and seeing how blue the water was. I remember watching U.S. and Japanese ships coming in and out of the port and wondering what it's like to live on one.

"It's not as fun as it looks, buddy," Dad would tell me.

The pier to the left of us caught Kaili's eye and she gasped.

"Can we sit at the end of it? Like, over the water?" She asked. She grabbed my arm and I swear she looked just like she did when we were little and she hit a baseball I pitched to her.

We walked all the way to the edge of the pier and sat with our feet dangling over the ocean. From our spot, we could see the public beaches and tons of people running and swimming in the water. One particular bunch of people were taking a group photo with matching shirts on.

"I wonder what that's like." Kaili swung her feet back and forth and kept her focus on the particularly large family.

"What?" I asked, picking at a split in the wood beside my thigh. I dropped the piece of wood between the cracks and watched it hit the water.

"Having a big family like that. I don't think we ever had a big family around us growing up. It was usually just us and Mom and Dad." Her feet stopped swinging and she looked down at the water. She brought her hands to her lap and started picking at her fingernails.

"We saw our grandparents every once in a while," I cowered down at the sudden shift in our conversation. I didn't want to have too deep of a conversation, but clearly I was out-ranked.

"Barely. I don't even remember what they looked like." She looked back at me and squinted her eyes at the harsh sun light.

"Wait, didn't you live with Grandma and Grandpa until you turned eighteen?" She asked quickly.

"Well, yeah, but I was never at the house. I stayed out more than I stayed in. I regret it now, but that's just how I was. I wasn't the best grandkid, I guess."

The last time I remember visiting Grandma and Grandpa with Kaili was when I had just turned ten and she was seven. We never really did spend much time with our grandparents or any of our cousins. Mom and Dad were both only-children, so all of our cousins were distant relation. Our great aunts and great uncles never visited or asked about us. I don't know if it was because of our parents or if they just genuinely didn't care.

"The tour crew is like a big family. Everybody knows everything about each other. We know everyone's strengths and weaknesses. We know what makes each other mad or happy and are just there for each other. Same way with Tanner, Lia, and Nat. Sure it's not a blood family, but still a family. It makes my life easier knowing that I always have them to run to."

I copied her actions and started picking at my fingernails as I spoke. She listened intently and took a deep breath.

"I wish I had that," she whined. I turned my body so I was completely facing her and shrugged my shoulders playfully.

"I'll share mine," I smiled and she looked over at me.

I could tell she was trying not to smile, but I wasn't having it. I made just about every funny face I could think of. It took me making a completely straight face before she finally smiled, making us both laugh.

Kaili and I stayed on that pier for at least two hours just talking. We talked about our fears, our dreams, and our experiences. I talked about recording my albums and touring around the world. I told her all about the different countries I had visited and the weird foods I was dared to eat by Tanner.

She told me everything she could remember about the basement. She remembered one day where she almost escaped, but Anthony Ross caught her with half her body out of the window. That's the day he boarded it up, she told me. She also told me about the dreams she's been having since she was found and how Tanner has helped her through some of them.

We talked about anxiety, how we've both battled it, and how today's world is trying to romanticize it. I told her about the day I was put on the medication and how bad my anxiety attacks used to be and she told me she only had anxiety attacks when the entire house was silent. Silence freaks her out, which I completely understood. I've never been a fan of silence myself.

One topic I could tell she was trying to avoid was her developing baby bump. She's scared. We both are, but I told her we could tackle it together.

Metaphorically speaking, of course. She made me promise not to tackle her baby when it's born.

"I don't know if I ever showed you this, but I've had it either on my neck or in my pocket since the day I was taken." Kaili reached into her shorts pocket and pulled out a long chain. At the end of the chain was a military tag. Dad's military tag.

"How did you get this?" I gasped, taking it into my fingers to look at it. All of his information was stamped into the metal and I fought the tears threatening to spill from my eyes.

"Dad gave it to me while you guys were playing basketball the day I was taken. He told me to hold it for him and keep it safe," she wept. She wiped away a tear from her cheek and sniffled. I remember Dad having to get a new one, but I assumed he had lost this one.

"It's my good luck charm," she sniffled.

I felt a strange sense of peace as we sat in silence; like nothing could ever hurt us again. Anthony Ross is in prison, we have Mom's stuff, Dad's military tags are around Kaili's neck, and God's on our side. What else could we ask for? Sure, we could ask for Mom and Dad to be here with us, but I know everything happens for a reason and that they're watching over us. We're okay.

# forty
## Kaili

We managed to spend the entire trip at the private beach without getting sunburned before we had to leave Florida. I absolutely loved every part of it and hated that it was ending. The worst part about leaving was packing up our week worth of dirty laundry into a suitcase.

"We'll just wash them when we get to Atlanta," Mark convinced me while I scrunched my nose at his smelly basketball shorts in a pile on the floor.

When we got to Atlanta, Mark had Dave and Tanner pick us up. His house was quite a ways away from the airport, so I attempted to nap on the way. That idea was quickly shot down when Mark heard one of his older songs on the radio.

"When I went to Europe for the first time, a mob of fans were waiting outside the airport and they were singing every word to this song together. It was amazing. I wish you could have seen it," he told me while he bobbed his head with the beat of the song.

"European girls are so hot." Tanner added, sticking his tongue out and pretending to drool all over himself. I wish I could have experienced those things with my brother, but at the same time I'm glad he and Tanner were able to experience them.

The house we pulled up to was so much bigger than Mark told me it would be. For lack of better words, *it was freaking huge*. I gawked at the size of it and tried my best not to run inside and explore.

"Welcome home, kid," his voice came from beside me. He threw his arm over my shoulder and looked up at the house.

"This is home?" My fingers fumbled with my sweatshirt sleeves. I really need to wash this thing. It's starting to smell weird.

"Well no, not really. It's never really had a *home-y* vibe, but it's nice. We have a huge pool, a basketball court, a studio, and a grand piano. Maybe after a while it will feel like home," he spoke highly of the place, but there was a hint of sadness in his voice.

Mark led me inside and showed me the living room. The place is twice as big on the inside, if that's even possible. Every part of it was slick and clean and, well, *boring*. There were no pictures on the walls. No paint; all of the walls white. All the furniture was black and expensive looking.

"There's no color in here."

My voice echoed off the walls. Tanner dropped my suitcase beside my feet and straightened his back. His spine popped and we both cringed at the noise.

"Yeah, we haven't exactly had time to paint it. We could hire someone to do it, but that takes the fun out of it," Tanner explained. Mark shot him an angry glare and I smiled.

"You're still mad about me throwing that bucket of paint on you last year when we painted your room, aren't you?" Tanner asked him. I giggled as he puffed up his chest at Mark. Mark shook his head.

"That was uncalled for, man. The paint was freezing and smelled really bad," he pointed his finger accusingly at Tanner.

They bickered for a few more minutes and I started roaming around the house. Eventually, I found the room I'm assuming is Mark's. The door was propped open with an old shoe and all the walls were red.

"Do you like it?" I flinched at the sound of Mark's voice behind me. He smiled at me and stood beside me, looking around the large room.

"Yeah. I like the red," I told him. I attempted to pull my sweatshirt off, but ended up getting stuck somehow. Mark chuckled, but helped me get it the rest of the way off my body and wadded up before throwing it in a dirty clothes basket.

"This is where I keep all my awards," he pointed to a corner of the room. He walked towards a door and opened it, revealing a collection of fancy clothes.

"You keep them in your closet?" I raised an eyebrow questioningly and he smirked, pushing the clothing to the side. Behind was a black door with a keypad lock on the door.

"If anyone in the media or any of my fans saw me do that, they'd accuse me of copying some old TV show but I wasn't the one who built the house."

He pushed it open and flipped a light switch before taking my hand and leading me inside. The space was small, much like a short hallway. There was a glass wall in front of us with rows and rows of shiny awards and plaques.

"This was originally a storm shelter, but there's an even bigger shelter in the basement so I remodeled this one and made it my little trophy room. See those? Those are my Grammy awards I was telling you about."

He named off every award and what he did to win them. Grammys, Music Television and Movie Awards, American Music Awards, Billboard Awards, and everything in between. He even had a few Country Music Awards for a song he wrote for a country band I couldn't remember the name of.

"Oh yeah, and this," he brushed past me and went towards something I hadn't noticed in the back corner. He grabbed a black case and popped it open. He pulled a guitar out of it and smiled at it.

"This is the first guitar I ever bought. I used this old thing to busk in the streets like I told you about. I named her Louise," he smiled as he held it.

The guitar was old and obviously worn down. There were broken strings sticking out from the top and a split in the wood near the hole on the front. Mark put the strap around his neck and started strumming the strings with his bare fingers.

"She's a little out of tune, but still good," he smiled down at Louise as his fingers worked over the strings. He played the tune of a song I remember Mom playing for us when we were younger. I couldn't remember the name of the song or any of the words, but I knew without a doubt it was the song I was thinking of.

"Hey guys, Kaili's room is ready," Tanner poked his head in the door and Mark stopped playing. He carefully placed Louise over his back and we followed Tanner out of the room. He stopped in front of a door down the hall and rubbed his hands together.

"Are you excited to see your room? It's not much but we can go shopping for more stuff that you like later." Mark bit his lip after he finished.

"I'm sure whatever it is, it's more than I could ask for," I assured them. My brother wrapped his arms around me and squeezed me.

"Alright, open it," he nodded to Tanner, letting go of me and facing me towards the room.

The walls were a light blue and empty. There was a massive bed with black sheets and a dark blue blanket on it. There was also a desk and closet, but my favorite part had to be the massive windows lining the front wall that looked out over the smoggy city of Atlanta.

"And I have a surprise for you," Tanner sang, walking to my new closet and pulling out a large box wrapped in black and white gift paper. He scooted it across the carpet and left it in front of me. My hands hesitantly touched the top of it before looking up at the only two men I will ever need in my life.

"Go on, kid. Open it," Tanner smiled and bounced on his toes in excitement. Mark looked over at him and cocked his head to the side.

"You didn't tell me you got her something," he whispered to him, lifting Louise over his head and gently leaning it up against the wall.

"Just trust me," Tanner whispered back and I rolled my eyes at their failed attempt to be quiet.

The paper ripped easily and I tried to stack it in a neat pile, but it toppled over. The tape holding the box closed proved to be more of a hassle than it seemed worthy at the time and eventually Tanner tore it off for me. I lifted the flaps and found a bunch of crumpled up paper.

"Tip it over," Tanner crossed his arms and smiled down at me. I did as he instructed, noticing just how heavy it was.

"Here, let me help you," Mark stepped up and dumped out the contents on the floor. Once I moved most of the paper off of it, I saw a large blank piece of wood with two small hooks connected to opposite ends of a wire laying in front of me.

"What is it?" I looked up at Tanner and he was biting his lower lip and scratching the back of his neck.

"Here, let's flip it over." Mark crouched down and helped me lift the heavy piece before flipping it right side up.

In front of me sat the desk top I was all too familiar with. The wood looked a bit darker than I remembered it and the surface was visibly smoother. The tally marks were more defined and the word *FREE* seemed shinier than I remember.

"Tanner," my voice came out in a gasp. Mark sat down on the floor beside me and lifted it onto our laps.

"I cleaned it up and sealed it with a wood sealant so it would look nicer. I figured it meant something to you," he mumbled.

I couldn't speak. My throat felt like it completely shut and I was fighting the tears threatening to fall from my eyes. Mark ran his hand over the top and I watched his lip start to quiver.

"I put the wire on the back so we can hang it up on the wall if you want," Tanner pointed at the desktop and stuffed his hands in his pocket.

"When did you work on it?" Mark looked up at Tanner and he sat on the floor in front of us.

"While you guys were still in Florida. If you don't like it, Kaili, we can burn it or something. But I just… I thought it would be a good thing to give you. Like a good reminder of how long you survived down there and how you're free now."

My fingers stayed over FREE. I spent 98 months destroying the surface of this piece of wood. Almost eight years spent in complete terror. Every day…no…every second that passed I wished and prayed to be free, but I honestly didn't think it would happen.

Mark stood up abruptly and left the room, returning a less than a minute later with a tool in his hand.

"Help me out here, bud," his request was directed at Tanner. I kept my eyes on the markings on the desk top, dazed.

Tanner assisted Mark in whatever he was doing, making a bunch of noise in the process. Before I knew it, the boys took the desk top from my hands

231

and hung it on the wall. Mark hauled me up off the floor and stood beside me.

I wiped under my eyes and took a deep, shaky breath. Tanner came and stood on the other side of me and held my small hand in his. Mark's arm snaked around my waist and I laid my head on his shoulder. Looking up at the desk top, I felt completely safe and secure.

And it was marvelous.

# **Acknowledgements**

Who would have thought that writing down a simple idea could lead to this? I certainly didn't. I didn't think I'd ever finish the darned thing, but I am so glad I did. This proves to me that I can do anything I set my mind to.

Mom and Dad, thank you for believing in this crazy dream of mine. You two have taught me that it's okay to be weird and expressive. You believed in me against all the nay-sayers. You've supported everything I've done from dropping out of college to quitting three jobs. I love you guys so much more than you realize.

Quincy, thank you for being the greatest big brother in all of creation. We've had ups and downs, but we always stick together and I can't thank you enough for all you've done for me. Not only have you been amazing, but you also gave me a wonderful sister-in-love, Erin, who has had nothing but endless love and acceptance for me. I love you both and can't wait to see you again.

My squad, you guys rock. You've listened to my endless rants and read crappy writings at three in the morning and I can't explain how blessed I am with you guys. You let me express myself with no judgement and that's all I could ever wish for. Thank you for letting me be me and loving me anyway. I guess I love you guys too.

To all of my family and friends, thank you for your support and kind words. Hearing that my writing makes other people excited for more makes me the happiest kid in the world.

26829109R00133

Made in the USA
Middletown, DE
07 December 2015